ROMANY ROSE

When Lucy Lee's grandparents reveal a shocking secret from her childhood, her world changes dramatically. She begins a new life, far removed from the outdoor living that is a Romany's, and is separated from her beloved Jasper Petulengro. Lucy learns to be a lady, and receives an offer of marriage from the Reverend Clement Orton. But the rakish Ronan Ivory also has plans for her . . . Can she leave the past behind — along with her true love?

CATRIONA McCUAIG

ROMANY ROSE

Complete and Unabridged

LINFORD
Leicester

First published in Great Britain in 2006

First Linford Edition
published 2007

British Library CIP Data

McCuaig, Catriona
    Romany Rose.—Large print ed.—
Linford romance library
1. Love stories
2. Large type books
I. Title
823.9'14 [F]

ISBN 978–1–84617–721–7

Published by
F. A. Thorpe (Publishing)
Anstey, Leicestershire

Set by Words & Graphics Ltd.
Anstey, Leicestershire
Printed and bound in Great Britain by
T. J. International Ltd., Padstow, Cornwall

This book is printed on acid-free paper

1

Lucy Lee gave herself up to Jasper's lingering goodnight kiss, sorry that their happy evening together had come to a close. She was reluctant to leave his fireside and looked forward to the time, not many months in the future, when they would be wed, never to be parted again. Overhead, the sky was dotted with stars, and somewhere an owl hooted.

Here and there other fires glowed softly and strains of music floated across the common. People were making the most of the fine evening after a week of mist and drizzle had caused misery to all the travellers. At this moment, life was good.

Lucy crept closer to her grandparents' caravan, attracted by raised voices. Something must be really wrong, she thought. She had never known them to be out of sorts with each other, but now there was definitely something amiss. Ezra Lee's voice was low and firm; his wife's high-pitched and pleading.

Lucy's bare feet were numb with cold from contact with the dew and she began to shiver. She knew she should go inside her own van and curl up under the blankets until her body recovered its warmth, but something made her stay, straining her ears to hear more.

'There are matters to be put right before I go,' Ezra said, It was impossible to make out his wife's reply, but Lucy knew about the stitch in his side that made him double over in pain from time to time, pain which could not be helped by any of Mariah's herbal remedies. Although he had not said as much to Lucy, reason told her that her beloved grandfather had not long to live, and the thought devastated her. Now it seemed that Ezra was confirming that fact.

'After she is wed,' Mariah cried now.

'That will be time enough. Please, Ezra, listen to me. She must not be taken from us. Once she is Jasper's bride, nobody can take her away.'

'She must be given the choice,' Ezra said sternly. 'That is only right.'

Obviously they were discussing her. Without a second thought, Lucy stepped out of the shadows and confronted the pair.

'You're talking about me, aren't you?' she demanded. 'Who wants to take me away from here? What is this choice I'm to be given?'

'We were not speaking of you at all,' her grandmother snapped. 'And haven't I always told you that listeners hear no good of themselves?'

Lucy smiled in the darkness. Mariah had given herself away with that last remark.

'Come and sit down, child. I had not meant to tell you yet, but now that you are here . . . ' Ezra moved over, patting the step beside him. Lucy sidled past the dying embers of their fire and sat

3

down at his side.

Mariah stood nearby, her arms folded. 'Tell your story, then, old man, and don't blame me when it all goes wrong.'

'Speak the truth and shame the devil,' he quoted, shaking his head sorrowfully. He turned to his grand-daughter. 'You don't remember your parents, of course, my child.'

Lucy shook her head. She had been brought up by her grandparents, having been told years ago that her father had left England when she was a baby, and that her mother had later died of consumption. She repeated this now.

'That is true enough, in its way,' Ezra nodded. 'Well, then. Petrel Lee was my son. I say was, for he was lost to me, although it may be that he still lives, out in Van Diemen's Land. He was caught setting snares in the woods to catch coneys, and condemned to transporta-tion for poaching, though how these gentry can lay claim to ownership of wild beasts is beyond me!

'Petrel's wife, Kezia, was wild with grief, with only her baby daughter to console her. She kept saying that the child was all she had left of Petrel.'

'And that baby was me,' Lucy breathed. Ezra went on as if she hadn't spoken.

'The baby died. There had been scarlet fever in one of the villages we passed through, and some of the children in our band caught it. Kezia was so desperate that we feared what she might do, to harm herself. Mariah kept her quiet with herb possets for a time, but that could not go on forever, so that is when you came along. It is your story, Mariah. Tell the girl now.'

Bewildered, Lucy turned to her grandmother. Mariah swallowed hard and took up the story.

'We were camped near a village in the Forest of Dean. I had walked there, hoping to sell clothes pegs and perhaps to tell a fortune or two. There was a little street of shops there, and standing outside the greengrocery there was a very grand perambulator, with a little girl sitting in it, dressed all in fine clothes. The child was crying, and I was about to go to her when a young nursemaid came out of the shop and slapped the child, telling her to be quiet. Then she went inside again, flirting with a young man who was serving behind the counter.

'That made me think now unfair life can be. There was our Kezia, grieving for the baby she loved so much, and here was this little soul, dressed in fine clothes, but with nobody to care tuppence for it. I suppose her mother to be some fine lady who handed over her children to servants who ill-treated them, while she went driving out in a fine coach and played cards with her friends. Well, I knew I could put that to rights! I snatched up the child and hurried away before anyone could stop me.'

There was a long silence while Lucy digested this. 'You mean, I was that child? I'm not really your grand-daughter at all?'

'You are as much our granddaughter as any child of our blood could be,' Ezra intervened, 'but yes, what Mariah says is true. You were the baby she brought home, the child that saved poor Kezia's sanity.'

Lucy felt strangely detached from what she had just heard. It was as if this was another of the old folk legends which people repeated to each other on winter nights. Stories of fairies and demons, knights and gypsy kings. Stories to listen to, wide-eyed with wonder, fantasies to take away the harshness of daily living.

Surely this was another such tale, of a gorgio child stolen away by the Romanies, who surely had enough children of their own without making off with other people's. At any moment now, her grandfather would recount the next bit; but Ezra remained silent.

On the other side of the common she could hear the shrill voices of children, eager to get the last ounce of play time before their mothers shouted at them to get to bed. It was as if there was a play going on, a play in which she was not an actor, but the audience. 'Is this really true?' she asked at last.

'It is true,' Ezra confirmed.

'And now this man of mine wants to send you back to your own people,' Mariah said bitterly. 'To live in a fine house, far away from all those who love you. To perhaps marry some fine gentleman and never travel the roads again. Held captive like a singing bird in a wicker cage.'

Shocked as she was, Lucy couldn't help laughing at that. Marry a fine gentleman, indeed! Chance would be a fine thing. She knew well the opinion of such folks when it came to gypsies! They were people to be despised, to be driven away from the villages they approached. People who were often accused of poaching and stealing.

She reached over and took her grandmother's work-worn hands. 'I'll never leave you, you can depend on that. And I'm promised to Jasper, and I won't leave him, either.'

'It may not be for you to decide,' Ezra said. 'The pattern of our lives is cut out for us long before we are born. For reasons we cannot understand it may have been ordained that you should come to us, and by the same token you may be meant to return to your own people now.'

'You are my own people!' Lucy cried, yet at the back of her mind other thoughts were creeping in. Did she have a mother somewhere, who thought of her every day, wondering where she was or if she was still alive? She had no memory of Kezia Lee, who had died so long ago, so it was not hard to imagine this other woman and how she might be feeling, just like the lady of the legend, whose child was stolen by the fairies. She gave a choked sob.

'There! Now see what you've done, Ezra Lee! You've upset the child, and to what purpose? Do you mean her to go to those people in their fine house and beg them to take her in! Even supposing they believe such a tarra-diddle, would they want her now?'

'Mebbe not, but before she weds Jasper the child must have her chance to know who she really is. And what of her parents? Think, Mariah! Even if they turn her away they will at least know she still lives. It will give them peace of mind if nothing else.'

Bitter resentment welled up inside Lucy. They should have thought of that before! Kezia's happiness had been bought at the price of some other woman's pain. And why hadn't all this been explained long ago, as soon as Lucy was old enough to take it in? Now everything she had believed to be true about herself was washed away. These two beloved people were not related to her at all, but were thieves of the worst kind.

'Have you thought what will happen to you if this story comes out?' she demanded coldly. 'If they could sentence your son to transportation for snaring coneys, what will they do to you for this? They'll hang you, or at the very least shut you away for life.'

And for a Romany, being shut up behind prison walls would be a fate worse than death. Mariah gave a whimper of fear, followed by Ezra's murmur of reassurance, but Lucy had no wish to hear more. She got up and stumbled towards her own van, where she huddled under the blankets, fully dressed.

2

The next morning, Mariah Lee went about her work, carefully avoiding Lucy's eye. Ezra sat on the steps of his van, smoking his old clay pipe and looking into the distance. Unable to settle down to working on the basket she was weaving, Lucy flung it down and marched over to Jasper's van where he was brewing something over the fire, his eyes streaming from the smoke. His brother, Lark, was seated nearby, carefully fashioning clothes pegs which the women of the band would sell in due course.

'My grandfather has told me a terrible thing,' Lucy blurted.

'Oh, ah? And what might that be, then?' Jasper wiped his brow with the back of his hand, squinting down into the iron pot as he did so.

'He says I'm not their son's child at

all. Mariah stole me from the gorgios when I was a baby!'

'Oh, that!' Jasper seemed unconcerned, although Lark had dropped his knife and was listening, open-mouthed.

'You knew already! You knew, and you didn't tell me!' Lucy punched his shoulder, causing him to stagger back.

'Steady on, Lucy! You'll have me over. I didn't say because it wasn't my place to tell. Ezra took me aside and told me the story as soon as we agreed to wed. Said I had a right to know.'

'In case you weren't willing to marry a gorgio, I suppose!' The tears spurted from Lucy's eyes, but Jasper didn't notice.

'Nothing of the sort, my gal. He just wanted me to be prepared, that's all. Mebbe you won't want to marry me, now you know you're really a fine lady, eh?'

'I'm not a fine lady! And of course I want to marry you. I love you, don't I?'

Lark looked from one to the other, with calculation in his eyes. 'I wonder what's in it for us, then?'

His brother rounded on him. 'What's in it for you, you mean! What could be in it? Don't you be getting the idea that Lucy's people will welcome me as a son-in-law, so I can hand over some of their money to you!' He guffawed at the very idea. 'Welcome me straight into the village stocks, they would.'

'They might be willing to pay us to keep quiet about this,' Lark said. 'Very likely they have other children. All grown up by now, wanting to make good marriages. Pillars of the community, as they call it. Magistrates and ministers, mebbe. They wouldn't want it getting about that their sister is a gypsy, now would they?'

'Oh, yes? It's blackmail they call that! They'd haul us off to gaol before you'd finished getting the words out! And what about Ezra and Mariah, eh? What d'you think would happen to them?'

Lucy was thinking furiously. She wouldn't put it past Lark to come up with some plan to make money from her dilemma. There was something nasty about Lark. He had always been jealous of Jasper, and would stop at nothing to queer his pitch.

She was reminded of a hazelnut she had once cracked open, to find twin kernels. One as plump and juicy, the other thin and shrivelled. Jasper was tall and handsome. He had music in his soul and had only to hear a tune once before playing it again on his fiddle. He could be gentle and ride any horse ever born.

If ever a man had been given the wrong name, that was Lark. There was nothing blithe about him. And now he knew a secret which could bring trouble on them all. She cursed herself for having mentioned it in his hearing. She was in danger, too.

Remembering what Jasper had said, she could imagine her birth parents going to any lengths to keep their friends from finding out about her. They might even have her confined to a lunatic asylum if she turned up on their doorstep claiming to be their long-lost daughter.

She flew across the wet grass to where Ezra Lee still sat staring into space. 'Lark Petulengro knows about me, Grandad! He's going to make trouble for us, and I'm so afraid of what's going to happen!

'He means to go to these people — the ones you say are my real parents — and ask them for money to keep quiet about me. People who live in fine houses are powerful, aren't they? That's what you've always said. They'll send the peelers after us and you know what will happen then!'

Ezra puffed placidly at his pipe. 'And where will he go, young Lark?'

'What do you mean?'

'England is a big place, Lucy. How will he find these people when he doesn't even know their name?'

'But you told Jasper all about it.'

'Certainly I told him the story, but I said nothing about the place you came from. Your grandmother and me are the only ones who know that, child, and even we don't know the name of these folk.'

'You told me the Forest of Dean!'

'Mebbe I did, but there's no call for you to go mentioning that. And there again, that's a big place. All sorts of towns and villages in that part of the world, there are. So you're safe so long as you keep your mouth shut.'

Lucy digested this. 'But suppose somehow he did find out. Suppose when we were in that part of the world again he heard the story of a kidnapped baby. He'd know that was me.'

Ezra shook his had. 'Rich people aren't stupid, child. If a gypsy turned up claiming to know the whereabouts of the missing girl, they'd say he'd heard the tale and was only trying to turn it to his own advantage. They'd clap him in gaol for trying it on and in the meantime we'd be long gone.'

'I wish you'd never told me about all this, Grandad, nor Jasper, neither. What good will it do me now? If I go to those people they'll think the same about me as they would about Lark. I'd be a fool to try it.'

He sucked on his pipe. 'We have proof, Lucy.'

'What sort of proof?'

'Mariah will show you. But not a word to a soul, mind!'

Grumbling mightily, Mariah beckoned to Lucy to follow her inside the van. She pulled up the worn matting from the floor, disclosing an iron ring set in the floorboards. There was a similar hidey-hole in Lucy's van where she kept the few coins which made up her meagre savings.

Reaching inside, the old woman pulled out a worn bag which she laid on the bed. Lucy watched, fascinated, as, one by one, Mariah placed an article of baby clothing on her lap.

A small velvet coat with a matching bonnet trimmed with white fur. A white dress adorned with many ruffles, and several items of underclothing such as Lucy couldn't put a name to. No gypsy child ever had so many garments. It was a wonder that any child could even breathe, weighed down by so many layers. Last of all came a tiny pair of shoes fashioned from the softest kid.

'You were wearing these when you were found,' Mariah murmured, smoothing the little coat with her hand. 'It grieved me to have to hide them away but we couldn't risk them being seen, you see. Oh, I know that people give us old clothes when we go begging from door to door but these might have been recognised.

'I'm sure there was a hue and cry after they found the child gone, and a description of her and the clothes she was wearing would be circulated. If Ezra has his way now and you go back to your own people, these things will prove who you are.'

'Put them away,' Lucy urged, looking over her shoulder as if she expected to find Lark peering in at them. 'Nobody must see these things until we decide what to do.'

'And if I have my way, you'll do nothing.' Mariah nodded, carefully folding the little garments and stowing them away in the burlap bag.

Over the next few days, Lucy said little to Jasper and, sensing her distress, he said nothing in return. She was aware of Lark's eyes on her and she was afraid. It was no secret that he wanted her for his bride although whether it was because he loved her after his own fashion, or simply wanted what his brother had, was anybody's guess.

Since she had turned him down, would he try to take his revenge now that the opportunity had arisen?

Now that she knew her true story, certain things which had puzzled her in the past fell into place. Her lack of skill in the telling of fortunes, for instance. Mariah made a good income from that and had tried to pass the knowledge on to her granddaughter. Lucy could read palms well enough; there was no mystery there. Each line meant something and all she had to do was to recognise those and describe what they meant. How many times a woman would marry; how many children she might have.

But it was in reading the cards that she fell short. Mariah had a special gift which meant she could see into the future, although she seldom gave bad news to her customers. After all, who wanted to pay out good money to hear that they'd be dead in childbirth within the year? But this gift, usually passed down the female line, had not been granted to Lucy Lee, and now she knew why.

She realised that in order to be a whole person, she needed to know more about her background, even though she had no intention of ever taking up the life which should have been hers. Although her mind was full of fear, she knew that she could never rest until she had traced her birth parents and had seen for herself the house where she was born.

3

Over the next few days Lucy gave a lot of thought to her situation, sometimes telling herself that she would leave well alone, but at others consumed with curiosity about her birth family. Strangely, it was Jasper who insisted that she should try to contact these people before they were wed.

'You mean we should try to get money out of them,' she snapped. 'Can't you see how that will bring trouble down on our heads? What will become of my poor grandmother if these people send the peelers after her? How could you even suggest such a thing, Jasper?'

He held up his hand to stem the flow of words which continued to pour out of her mouth. 'No, no, my love! That is Lark's idea, not mine. I am not such a fool as to think we could try that and get away with it.'

'Then what are you saying?' Lucy was still not mollified.

'I am in agreement with Ezra, that's all. It's best that you know what you are missing before you wed me. If you go back to your old life you could be wearing silks and satins, and sleeping in a goose feather bed, eating meat every day and going about in a fine coach.'

'I don't care for any of that. It's you I love, Jasper. I'd go to the ends of the earth with you. Fine clothes and such mean nothing compared with that.'

He put his arm around her and kissed the top of her head. The smell of wood smoke filled his nostrils.

'Ah, love, would you feel the same ten years from now, cold and starving on a wet winter's day, with half a dozen young 'uns around your skirts? Would you turn against me then, thinking of what might have been?'

'I'd never turn against you!' she cried, but he shook his head.

'You must first find out what you'd be missing and then, if it's me you choose, we can go forward with no regrets.'

'They might not want to have anything to do with me,' Lucy reminded him, thinking of the many times she had knocked on a cottage door, trying to sell clothes pegs or offering to read palms, only to have the dogs set on her.

'Then you will know where you stand,' he said.

'We'll reach the Forest by June, I reckon,' Ezra said, when they went to him with their decision.

'And will we camp near the place where they live, Grandad?'

'Nay. We'll stop a few miles away, within riding distance. You and Jasper can ride over to Briarwood by yourselves. That way, you have a good chance of getting away fast if things go wrong, and the authorities won't know where to look for the rest of us if they hope to track us down.'

'I'm afraid, Grandad. They'll drive us

from the door before we get a chance to explain.'

'You do have Mariah's proof,' he reminded her, 'although that could be snatched from you by some servants before you even meet the master of the house.' He thought for a moment. 'Then you must go to the nearest church, and ask to speak to the vicar there. He will know if your parents are still alive, and can act as go-between. Say you will come a second time, bringing the proof with you. It is a risk, but one which has to be taken.'

In June the band crossed over into Gloucestershire and in due course set up camp in a meadow near the village of St Briavel's.

'Why are we stopping here?' Lark asked suspiciously. 'There'd be better pickings farther on, in a bigger place. By the look of some of the folks hereabouts they've only the clothes on their backs, so why buy clothes pegs if they've nothing to put out on the wash line?'

'Quarter day is coming up,' Ezra replied. 'There's to be a hiring fair, and Mariah reckons there'll be plenty of young maids as wants their fortunes told. No point in missing a chance like that.'

'S'pose I could pick a few pockets, then,' Lark muttered, still not wholly convinced.

At dawn the next morning, Jasper mounted his black horse and helped Lucy up behind him, and they left the camp before most people were awake. Some hours later they arrived at Briarwood, which was a pretty village not much larger than St Briavel's.

The church was not hard to find because of the tower which was visible from all directions. St Mary's had been built in the days when the Norman conquerors were busily establishing themselves throughout England, although to be sure Lucy knew nothing of that.

Her formal education had been sketchy to say the least, although she could identify almost every bird and flower that she came across in her travels, and had a good knowledge of herbs, gleaned from Mariah.

'Do I go in there and look for the vicar?' Lucy wondered, her voice trembling slightly.

'Looks like the place is deserted at this time of day,' Jasper continued. 'Best go to the vicarage and ask. It's likely that house next to the grave-yard.'

'Come with me, then?' she pleaded, but he shook his head.

'No, I'll stay here with the horse. Anything goes wrong, you get back here as fast as you can, and we'll be off like lightning.'

And so, fighting down the nausea which threatened to overpower her, Lucy went up the flagstone path between borders of gaily-coloured flowers, and raised her hand to knock on the door.

She looked back at Jasper, who waved encouragingly.

The door was flung open by a large woman who stared her down while she delivered a speech which time had obviously perfected.

'We don't want no pegs, we don't want none of our chickens stolen, and I don't want my palm read, neither. This is a Christian household, this is!'

'What is it, Fanny?' A man's voice was heard, coming from somewhere inside the house.

'Just some gyppo, Vicar. She's just leaving.' She made to shut the door, but Lucy was too quick for her. Pushing the woman aside she ran in the direction of the voice and found herself in a room filled with books. A man in a black cassock was seated at a small roll-top desk, writing on a pad of paper with a quill pen.

'I tried to stop her, sir, but she pushed right by me!' the housekeeper panted, tugging at Lucy's arm.

'I don't mean no harm, but I have to speak to you, sir!' Lucy pleaded. 'It's real important. Please hear what I have to say!'

The vicar put down his pen. 'Very well, then. I suppose I can spare you a few minutes. That will be all, thank you, Fanny.'

The woman flounced away, closing the door behind her with a bang.

'Sit down then, girl,' the vicar invited, removing a pile of books from the only other chair within sight. 'Are you in some kind of trouble?'

Lucy took a deep breath. 'I was wondering — are there any people round here who lost a little girl years ago?'

He smiled at her over his glasses. 'A great many, I should say, child mortality being what it is. Why, I myself lost a child, and my own wife too, who did not survive childbirth. You have only to look at the gravestones outside to attest to that.'

Lucy gulped. 'No, I mean really lost, not dead. I, um, heard a story about a baby who went missing from her perambulator when her nursemaid wasn't looking. I wondered if that was true.'

She had his attention now. 'Why, yes. A terrible case, to be sure. It was soon after I came to Briarwood. It was the Ingrams' only child, little Lucinda was her name.'

Lucinda! Mariah must have heard the maid calling her that, and decided on a more homely form of the name to avoid suspicion.

'I think that was me!' Lucy blurted. The vicar frowned.

'A likely story! This is not the first time the Ingrams have heard from people claiming to be their lost daughter. Wicked people, attempting to profit from the grief of others. And if you are one of them, you'll see the inside of the gaol before sunset if I have anything to say about it!'

Lucy was terrified, but she stood her ground. 'I have proof, sir. The clothes I was wearing when I was taken by the gypsies. Mrs Ingram will recognise them, I expect.'

'Hand them over, then, and I'll undertake to show them to the Ingrams.'

Lucy shook her head. 'I haven't brought them with me. If you speak to these people on my behalf, I'll come back tomorrow.'

Many thoughts seemed to be chasing through the vicar's head, but at last he nodded. 'Very well. I shall leave at once for Briarwood Hall and, if he is at home, tell Mr Ingram what you have told me, but I can't guarantee any favourable result. These poor people have suffered many disappointments over the years, and his wife is an invalid now. Understandably, she has never recovered from the loss of her child.'

Lucy went out to join Jasper, telling him in a low voice what had happened.

'Do you think he meant what he said? What if he's gone to fetch the magistrate instead?'

Jasper shrugged. 'Nothing else to do but wait and see,' he muttered.

'Where is everybody? Oh, Jasper,

they've gone!' Lucy looked around their campground with astonishment. Had they come to the wrong place? Were their people waiting just around the next bend in the road?' They had returned to tell Ezra and Mariah what had happened, but what were they supposed to do now?

She turned to Jasper. 'You knew about this, didn't you? You knew, and you didn't tell me! How could you, Jasper. How could you!' she pummelled his chest with her fists and he pulled her close to him, murmuring soft words. She had seen him gentle a fractious horse in such a way.

'Do you think I'd have brought us all this way if I'd known?' he said, when she was quiet at last. 'I'm as shocked as you, but not surprised.'

'But why? How could they do it to us?' She blinked back the tears as she spoke.

'I can understand it, my love. Ezra truly wants you to meet your parents and he knows how hard it will be for you. There can be no turning back now when we have no means of following. As for the rest of the band, why, they've taken themselves out of harm's way, I don't doubt. Even after so many years your father may seek revenge, and who knows what form that revenge may take? These gorgios have power, my love. You know what happened to Petrel, and all he stole was a coney, not a gorgio child.'

'But what about you, Jasper? What will you do now?'

'No need to worry about me. I'll stay nearby until I see you're all right, and then I'll be on my way. I'll meet up with the rest at the gathering place, if not before.'

Now the tears streamed down her face as if they would never stop, for it was only a matter of days since she had gone about blithely, looking forward to their wedding at that very place.

'Then we'll go away together now,' she gulped. Jasper shook his head.

'These things are written in the stars,

as well you know. Hasn't Mariah taught you that? What will be, will be. Besides, haven't you thought about your parents? By now they may have been told that you are alive and well, and they will be overjoyed at the thought of seeing you again. Could you be so cruel as to dash their hopes a second time?

'I know that Mariah acted for the best all those years ago, but in her sorrow for the death of her own grandchild she gave no thought to the feelings of your poor mother. True, the woman gave you into a servant's keeping, but that did not mean she cared nothing for you. That is the way of rich gorgios, or so I've heard.'

Lucy shook her head, thinking as she did so that they might well be the ones to reject her! People had a low opinion of gypsies and the thought of letting one stay under their roof was horrifying. They'd be afraid she might run off in the night, carrying the family silver. The Ingrams had had many years to come to terms with losing their daughter and had probably come to the conclusion that she was dead and gone.

As the vicar had suggested, they might suspect some trick. Stories such as that of the disappearance of a child belonging to wealthy people became local legends, to be told in the inns on winter nights. Strangers could hear those tales and decide to turn the situation to their own advantage.

'We'd best turn around now and go back as far as we can while there's still light,' Jasper decided. 'Then we'll find some place to spend the night — a cosy hay rick, mebbe — and rest the horse.'

This made sense, for they had no lantern to see by. All their belongings had gone with the band, except for Lucy's bundle which contained the all-important baby clothes and some bread and cheese.

In the morning they would go back to the vicarage and then, for better or for worse, Lucy's future would be decided.

*   ★   ★

'I've brought the proof,' Lucy told the vicar, when she was seated in his study once again. This time he had greeted her more kindly, and even Fanny had been marginally more pleasant when she had opened the door.

'All in good time,' the vicar replied, looking at her with a pained expression on his austere face. She had washed in a fast-flowing stream and combed her hair, but there had been nothing she could do about her shabby dress and battered boots. She would rather have gone barefoot as usual but that had seemed inappropriate for the occasion.

'Mr Ingram's solicitor will be here shortly, and he will decide what happens next, Miss um, Lee.'

Lucy sat on the edge of her chair, holding her shawl tightly around her. She hoped she wasn't going to be sick. That would be the final indignity.

As before, she let her gaze wander

around the room, looking at the leather-bound books, the paintings of wild highland scenes, and the portrait of the young Queen Victoria. This must be how the rich lived, surrounded by things which were not essential to life.

If the Reverend Arthur Brown had been able to read her mind he would have laughed aloud, for the living was barely enough to sustain him and his curate, and pay the wage of their housekeeper. The expression 'poor as church mice' was no idle boast.

The solicitor arrived, clad in a frock coat and top hat. He refused the offer of a glass of Madeira — no refreshment had been offered to Lucy — and suggested that they get down to business immediately. Trembling, Lucy unwrapped the little garments and waited for his reaction.

It was Mr Brown who spoke first. 'Of course, these things of themselves prove nothing. They could have been obtained from any second hand clothes stall in the market. And would the

Ingrams recognise the things their child was wearing, after all these years? Some nursemaid would have dressed the infant that day and the parents would have no idea what was put on her.'

Lucy was furious. 'I'm not a liar!' she bleated. 'I didn't want to come here in the first place! My grandfather made me. He hasn't long to live and he says he wants this to be put right before he goes. I've done what he said so if you don't believe me I'll go, and good day to you!'

She rose to her feet but the solicitor put up a hand to stop her and she subsided.

'At the time of the child's disappearance, a description of her clothing was circulated in the newspapers and on posters. A copy of such a publication is on file in our chambers, and I must say that the description tallies with what I see here.' He pursed his lips. 'Of course, as you say, Mr Brown, that is not positive proof. These may well be the missing clothes without this being the young lady in question. It is useless to speculate how we may have one without the other; the final decision as to whether this is indeed Miss Lucinda will be up to Mr Ingram himself.'

The vicar cleared his throat. 'When I called upon Mr Ingram yesterday he explained that his daughter was fair-complexioned, with blue eyes and fair hair.'

He looked meaningly at Lucy, with her dark curls and sun-browned skin. Lucy thought it best not to mention that when she had first arrived at the gypsy camp, Mariah had dyed her hair with tea; it was age that had darkened her hair permanently, just as it was exposure to wind and rain that coloured her skin to resemble that of the rest of the gypsy women.

The solicitor must have been satisfied that there was at least some chance of Lucy being the missing girl, for he showed her out to his carriage without further ado, saying that Mr Ingram wanted to meet her, and must not be kept waiting.

Reverend Mr Brown seemed disappointed when told that his presence wasn't required; being human he would have liked to be there when the drama unfolded.

When Briarwood Hall came into view, Lucy was overwhelmed by its grandeur. Nobody could have called it beautiful, but it had a certain stark elegance, with its portico over the main door, two windows on each side and seven windows above. Some sort of ivy or creeper covered part of the walls, softening the overall appearance of the house.

Smooth lawns flanked the circular gravel drive and when the solicitor's carriage stopped at the front door a liveried footman hurried down the steps at once. Obviously they were expected.

They were shown into the library, a room much like the vicar's study, but on a larger scale. Glancing at the leather-bound volumes Lucy wondered if anyone had actually read all those tomes or if they were just for show, like the paintings and ornaments she had glimpsed as they made their way through the house.

'So this is the girl who claims to be my daughter, is it?'

Lucy swung round to look at the man who had come noiselessly into the room. He was a tall man, dressed in beautifully-cut clothes and walking with the aid of a gold-topped cane. She had somehow thought that she would recognise him on sight, but somehow she felt nothing. He could have been any member of the gentry for all she knew.

She gazed back at him, her head held high.

'She has brought these clothes with her, Mr Ingram,' the lawyer said, placing the package on a mahogany desk. 'They appear to tally with the description of the garments worn by Miss Lucinda on the day of her disappearance. Not that this proves her identity conclusively, of course, as I explained to the vicar.'

'Come closer to the window,' Mr Ingram ordered. 'I wish to see you in the light. Yes, this girl is the image of my sister Emily, as she was at this age. There can be no doubt in my mind that this is my daughter. Welcome home, my child.'

Lucy heaved a sigh that was part relief, part apprehension. Her new life had begun.

4

'Take these downstairs and burn them!'
The housekeeper looked from the little
housemaid to Lucy's clothes with
distaste. In fact, the woman had not
viewed Lucy herself with much better
grace.

She was obviously torn between
offering her the deference due to Miss
Lucinda, the returned daughter of the
house, and showing the intruder to
the door as one of the despised race of
gypsies. Lucy knew she must begin as
she intended to go on.

Summoning all her courage she said.
'I want them washed and ironed, and
returned to me here, if you please.' She
was not at all sure that she intended to
remain here, and if it came to the point
where she had to leave, she wanted her
own clothes, not this fancy gown which
had belonged to Miss Emily before she

left the house to be married.

The housekeeper primed her lips and swept out, leaving the little maid to see to Lucy's needs.

'What is your name?' Lucy asked, liking the look of the young girl in the neat cap and apron.

'Annie, Miss.'

'Well, Annie, I'd love something to eat. I was too nervous to take food this morning, but I'm hungry now. do you think you could fetch me a nice strong cup of tea, and something to go with it?'

'Yes, Miss.' The girl scuttled off, her eyes wide. Lucy guessed that the rest of the staff would be full of questions. It wasn't every day that something like this brightened their lives of drudgery. Come to that, it wasn't every day of the week that she experienced such a strange happening, either. Well, as long as this lasted, she might as well enjoy it to the full, and see how the other half lived!

When Annie returned, staggering

under the weight of a tray containing a pot of tea and a plate of fruit cake, she announced that luncheon would be brought up at one o'clock.

'Mrs Hyndman says as how you're to meet the mistress at two, so you'd likely want to eat up here quiet like, before you go down.'

'Is Mrs Ingram ill, Annie? I did wonder why she didn't come to see me this morning.' This had puzzled Lucy very much, for although she had hardly expected the woman to fall on her neck the moment she walked through the door, it did seem strange. Surely she should have been eager to meet her long-lost daughter? Perhaps she was unable to believe it was true.

'The mistress is an invalid, Miss. She lies on her couch all day. she has Miss Meech, of course — that's her companion, that is — and ladies come to call but she never leaves the house. Hasn't for years.'

'Oh, dear. Does she suffer from a wasting disease?'

'I don't think so, Miss. They do say down in the kitchen . . . ' she broke off, looking over her shoulder. the house-keeper did not encourage the staff to gossip about their betters and Annie didn't want to get herself in trouble.

'Go on,' Lucy prompted. 'What is it they say in the kitchen?'

'Well, Miss, Cook says as how some ladies doesn't like that side of married life, giving birth and all that, so they sort of go into a decline so their husbands leave them alone. Cook says if they had to get up in the morning and scrub the floors they wouldn't have time for all that nonsense, but that's the gentry for you.

'They do say as the mistress went to pieces when her little girl was took, and has never been the same since. Not that you can blame her for that, can you?'

'So the Ingrams had no more children after that?' Lucy would have liked to have a sister or brother. 'How sad.'

'Some of them say downstairs, as the

46

mistress should have pulled herself together after a bit, for what's the point of going on grieving year after year? If you go up the churchyard there's plenty of children's graves there. People lose young'uns all the time. that's life, Miss.'

'At least those parents know where their children are! Mrs Ingram has gone all these years not knowing what happened to the baby. That must be worse.'

'Yes, Miss.' Annie spoke quietly but it was obvious from the expression on her face that she didn't agree. 'If there's nothing else you want, Miss, I'll get down to my dinner in the servants' hall.'

'Yes, yes, off you go.' Lucy picked up a slice of fruit cake and crumbled it in her fingers. Strangely enough she felt more nervous at the prospect of meeting Mrs Ingram than she had when she was introduced to her father. Perhaps because she remembered Kezia and thought of her as her mother rather than this unhappy stranger.

Promptly at two she went downstairs and knocked at the door of Mrs Ingram's suite. It was opened by the companion, Miss Meech. A sad-looking soul dressed in droopy grey garments. She ushered Lucy into a room over-crowded with furniture and knickknacks and so stuffy from lack of air that Lucy found it hard to breathe.

'Here is Miss Lucinda, Madam.'

Mrs Ingram raised a weary hand and indicated a chair near her couch. 'Do sit down, my dear. Did you have a good journey?'

Lucy answered a series of polite questions which meant precisely noth-ing. How was the weather? Had she seen any plays lately? Been to the opera? Been boating on the river? Lucy could think of a dozen things which might be more pertinent to the situation. Where had she lived? Who had looked after her? Had they been kind? But none of this was forthcom-ing.

'I had a little girl once,' Mrs Ingram

said, with a sudden change of tone. 'Where is that photograph, Meech? Bring it here, please?'

The companion got up and crossed to the fireplace, where a number of photos in silver frames stood on the mantel. She chose one which showed a younger Mrs Ingram, holding a baby on her lap. Lucy gazed at it with interest, trying to recognise herself in the person of the chubby baby.

'Yes, that's my Lucinda,' Mrs Ingram said proudly. 'She's not here now, and they don't know where she's gone.'

Lucy cleared her throat. 'Um, I'm Lucinda. I've come home.'

'Nonsense! My Lucinda is a baby, as you can very well see. What is more, she has lovely fair curls and you, you're as dark as a gypsy!' She turned to her companion. 'I must rest now, Meech. You'll see my visitor out, won't you?'

Baffled, Lucy stood up and prepared to leave. Mrs Ingram inclined her head graciously. 'Thank you for coming! Do call again!'

'I'm afraid this is not one of her good days,' Miss Meech whispered, as she ushered Lucy to the door. 'You mustn't mind too much, Miss Lucinda. After everything she's been through your coming home is too much for her to take in.'

Lucy mumbled something meaningless and fled upstairs. This was still a house of mourning, and what was the point of her being here? She was soon to find out.

'I gather that you received scant satisfaction when you met my wife this afternoon,' her father said, when they were sitting in the drawing-room that evening. 'It was no more than could be expected, considering the state of her health in recent years. She lives in the past, and believes that her child has only recently been taken from her. She is quite unable to reconcile that fact with the young woman you have become.'

'Perhaps I should go away again,' Lucy said, suddenly longing to be with

Ezra and Mariah, and of course Jasper.

'No indeed. You are my daughter, Lucinda, and I can only be grateful that you have been restored to us. God willing we can make it up to you for all the lost years and the advantages you have missed. You will eventually be able to take up your place in society, and in due course I shall find a suitable husband for you.'

'I shouldn't know what to do in society, Mr Ingram.' She thought it wise to keep quiet on the subject of husbands.

'You must call me Papa, my dear. That was the first word you learned to speak, but I daresay you've forgotten about that! As for taking your place in society, you have much to learn, so I shall engage a governess for you.'

'A governess! But aren't they for children?'

'In most cases, yes, but you will need someone to teach you the conventions of polite society. Table manners, the art of conversation, how to behave when young gentlemen come calling.'

'And how to breathe in corsets, and how to walk gracefully without tripping,' Lucy thought, looking down at her dress, which brushed the floor rather than showing her ankles, which was what she was used to. Suddenly she felt more cheerful. Being in society was like a game, and once you knew the rules all would be well.

Jasper followed at a safe distance as the carriage containing Lucy and the important looking gentleman left the vicarage and turned on to the main road. When they reached what he assumed to be Briarwood Hall he was obliged to trot on past when a woman emerged from the lodge and opened the great iron gates. He could not, of course, follow the carriage up the drive but at least he knew where Lucy had gone, and could get in touch later.

He returned the next afternoon. He tied his horse to a tree with the length of rope he always carried in his saddlebag, and with his poacher's cunning crept through the wood and climbed the wall leading into the grounds. From there he made his way to the back door and announced that he had a message for Miss Lucy.

'Is that so!' the cook sniffed. 'And what would Miss Lucy be wanting with the likes of you? Get off with you, before I call the men.'

'I was asked to deliver this note to her, for her eyes alone,' Jasper said, reaching into his waistcoat pocket and bringing out a grubby sheet. Not having any sealing wax he had been unable to close the folded paper, but with any luck the servants here could not read. He had had some basic schooling when the band had been in winter quarters, but it was not everyone who could afford the penny a week it cost to send a child to school.

He thrust the letter into the cook's hand and loped away, thinking it unwise to linger. She turned it over in her hand, wondering what to do, and still staring at it when the housekeeper entered the kitchen.

'I hope that isn't a love letter for one of the maids,' Mrs Hyndman snapped. 'You know how the master feels about followers. Give it here, Mrs Eaton.'

Cook handed it over silently, failing to mention that the fellow had asked for Miss Lucy. The poor girl was going to have enough trouble settling in here without Mrs Hyndman tattling to the master. There was no love lost between the two women, never had been.

'Just as I thought!' the housekeeper sniffed. ''Meet me after dark back of the lodge.' For whom was this intended, Mrs Eaton?'

'I don't know, I'm sure. The chap didn't get a chance to tell me. He took to his heels as soon as he saw you coming.'

'Well, I know what I'm going to do with it!' Mrs Hyndman threw the paper into the fire and watched with some satisfaction while it curled up and disappeared. The cook shrugged. She had enough to do without wasting time wondering what it was all about.

Jasper doubted whether Lucy would ever receive his note. He had been foolish to even try. Meanwhile, he had to find some legitimate reason for staying in the district. People were apt to get edgy if they saw strangers loitering about. He headed straight for the livery stable.

'Any chance of a job going, mate?' he asked when a burly man carrying a pitchfork and a tin pail emerged from a stable door.

'Not here, there ain't. I've got a full house as it is. Try over at Jarvis's. He might have something.'

'What's Jarvis's?'

'Ned Jarvis. Trains race horses. He won't take on just anybody, mind. Know much about horses, do you?'

'Enough,' Jasper agreed. 'Where is this Jarvis, then?'

The man jerked a thumb back the way Jasper had come. 'Go back till you comes to the crossroads. Turn left. And about two miles out you'll see some big white gates, and the stable's down the lane apiece from there.'

When Jasper reached the white gates he was surprised to see a man leaving the place carrying a bulging burlap bag. Since the fellow was on foot and Jasper was mounted, the man held the gate open for the horse to pass through.

'Hope you're not thinking of working for that devil of a Jarvis!' the man grunted. 'More fool you if you do!'

'What's wrong with him, then?'

'What's wrong with him! What isn't wrong with him? I could keep you standing here all day and I still wouldn't be done telling you. Always bawling at a fellow about something. Never satisfied, he isn't. Work, work, work! You can keep at it from six o'clock in the morning till dinner time but if he sees you stopping to catch your breath for a minute all hell breaks loose. Hits you over the shoulders with that blackthorn stick of his, soon as look at you!'

'Thanks for the warning, mister. I'll bear it in mind.'

The man trudged off, and Jasper urged his horse towards the stable yard. Before he had time to get his bearings he heard shouting coming from the direction of a small paddock, and the whinnying of a frightened horse. A great black stallion was plunging and stamping, and a heavy-set man was roaring at a stable hand to get the beast under control. Judging by the way the several onlookers were keeping their distance they were all afraid of the animal.

'Here, catch hold of this,' Jasper said, as he slid from his horse's back. He dodged under the fence rails and within seconds had approached the stallion, making soothing noises. The horse snorted and stamped but gradually simmered down.

'There's a poor old boy,' Jasper whispered, as he scratched the animal's nose, smiling as the ears came forward and the head lowered. Jasper gently took hold of the halter and prepared to lead the horse away.

'Where d'you want this 'un put,

mister?' he grinned, as the man in charge, who undoubtedly was Ned Jarvis, looked on in amazement.

'Put him back in his stall. One of the men will show you where.' He turned away, to berate somebody for work undone. Jasper was rubbing down the sweating animal, hissing softly through his teeth as he worked, when Jarvis came into the stable.

'Are you looking for a job, man?'

'Could be,' Jasper replied, not looking up.

'Three shillings a week, all found.'

'And feed for my horse, Mister?'

'Take off a shilling for that.'

'Sixpence.'

'Done!'

The money was a pittance, of course, but Jasper had achieved his aim, to stay near Lucy. He also had a roof over his head, out of the wet, even if was nothing more than a bed of straw in a loft with other men, and there was food for himself and Rajah. As for Jarvis himself, Jasper had defeated better men than him during his years on the road.

All he had to do was try to keep his temper so he wouldn't be dismissed for insolence, but he was used to that too. He often earned a few coins by helping with the harvest on the farms the band camped near to, and he had learned to tolerate a bad master and worse conditions by reminding himself that he was only bound for a short time. After the work was finished he was free to go on his way.

Ned Jarvis kept a racing stable. Some of the horses were his; a few belonged to other owners, who paid him to house and train the animals. Most of the men employed by Jarvis were stable hands like Jasper, but two were jockeys who actually rode the horses at race meetings.

He was pleased when Jarvis came to him one evening and announced gruffly that he was to ride out in the string the next morning. With any luck he could become a race jockey too, if he stayed on for a while.

5

The governess was a pleasant woman of some thirty years, Miss Deborah May by name. She explained to Lucy that she was the daughter of a clergyman who had contracted pneumonia one winter after getting soaked through while conducting a burial.

Within two weeks of that funeral he had joined his elderly parishioner in the graveyard. Miss May, who had kept house for her father since her mother's death some years before, now found herself homeless and had to go out to work.

'I was fortunate that your papa contacted me when he did,' she told Lucy. 'The children with whom I've been working for the past two years — twin girls — have now been sent to a boarding school for young ladies, so once again I found myself with nowhere to go.'

Used as she was to life on the road, Lucy couldn't quite understand the dread with which Miss May faced the thought of homelessness, but the older woman's shudder spoke for itself, and she murmured something which she hoped sounded sympathetic.

'I can see that we have no time to waste,' Miss May remarked. 'Autumn will be upon us soon and there will be balls and parties to attend. Your papa wishes you to be made ready for your debut into society then. Oh, I don't mean that you are to be presented at Court,' she amended, seeing Lucy's look of horror, 'but you have to be brought out in some way, if only to be introduced to the County.'

A long round of lessons followed, in which Lucy learned many things which she felt foolish and unnecessary. The use of cutlery was one such thing. Each course at a meal had its own knives, forks or spoons and it was daunting to come upon a place at table on which numerous implements were laid out. All her life she had eaten food with one tin spoon, and been none the worse for it!

She learned to walk daintily instead of striding out freely, and this was helped by the constricting garments she had to wear. Fortunately she was so slender that the dreaded corset held few terrors; where other women suffered agony when their flesh was pinched by whalebone she could breathe easily as long as she held herself upright.

'But always remember not to indulge too freely at table,' Miss May warned, 'or some unfortunate sound may escape.'

There were rules of dress. Some jewellery was unsuitable for day and might only be worn in the evening. Certain colours were prohibited. A lady might never venture out of doors without a bonnet and gloves, and when returning home after visiting the poor it was essential to remove one's clothing at once in case one had picked up fleas.

Lucy learned how to speak to members of the upper class, and how to address servants. Fortunately she was a quick learner and thought of this as a game. It was as if she was learning a part in a farce, put on by strolling players.

The first test came on the following Sunday, when everyone in the household, with the exception of Sophia Ingram and Miss Meech, went to church. Lucy followed Marcus Ingram down the aisle to the Ingram pew, which unfortunately was near the front of the church, which meant they had to pass the congregation. She felt that all eyes were on her.

The vicar wasn't present at the eleven o'clock matins, but a younger, fair-haired man was conducting the service in his place.

'That's the curate,' Miss May whispered. 'The Reverend Clement Orton.'

'How do you know him?' Lucy whispered back.

'He comes from my home parish. I am acquainted with the family.'

A stern look from Marcus Ingram

interrupted this exchange, and at that moment the organ peeled out and everyone stood for a hymn. Lucy noticed that the Reverend Orton's eye was upon them, and she wondered if he, like everyone else, was staring at her, or if perhaps he had recognised Miss May and was delighted to see her there. Perhaps there was something between them.

This idea was underlined the next morning, when Mr Orton came calling. He spent only a short time with Sophia Ingram and Miss Meech, and seemed glad to join Lucy and Miss May in the morning-room, where they plied him with tea and caraway seed cake. When he finally came to the point it seemed there was a need for sick-visiting at the cottages, which he felt could be undertaken by the young ladies of Briarwood Hall. As in most country places it was the inhabitants of the 'big house' who took broth and fruit to the needy but Lucy's mother had never done her duty in that regard.

'Of course it is impossible for poor Mrs Ingram to be of assistance, being an invalid,' Mr Orton said, 'but I feel sure that Miss Lucinda can be of service now, accompanied by you, Miss May.'

Glad of the prospect of getting out into the fresh air, Lucy agreed with enthusiasm, so the next day the pair of them set out with the pony and trap for some of the poorer homes in the village. She was amused to find the patients sitting up in bed with their eyes gleaming at her approach.

'It's so romantic,' one woman gushed, as she accepted the fruit compote and calves-foot jelly they had brought for her old father. 'Imagine, stolen by gypsies and now you've made your way home after all these years.'

'I remember when you was taken away, my dear,' the old man nodded. 'Left outside the village shop, you was, while that useless Polly Webb dallied with her sweetheart, cudding and kissing in the middle of the day.'

'I don't remember her,' Lucy replied. 'I wonder what happened to her?'

'Sent away with a flea in her ear, and no references, which was no more than what she deserved. If she'd been a gal of mine I'd have given her a good hiding, that I would. Leaving the poor little mite bawling in that there perambulator.'

At another cottage a housewife asked Lucy if she could read palms. 'I thought mebbe you learned that among the gypsies, dear? Me and my Tom, we've never had no children, but it's not too late. I thought mebbe you could tell me if there's any hope? Any hope at all?'

Lucy caught Miss May's disapproving look and concluded that she'd better not comply. She would have been happy enough to oblige but her governess was a clergyman's daughter and would look upon fortune telling as superstition.

'I'm afraid we don't have time today,' she murmured, trying not to notice the woman's look of disappointment. She wondered if she would ever truly fit in to the world into which she had been born. There were so many rules to be observed, and some of them seemed so silly. Why did these people have to make life so complicated? It was Queen Victoria's fault, she supposed. The monarch had brought up her family quite strictly — although she seemed to have failed where the Prince of Wales was concerned — and encouraged her people to follow her example.

On the way home their trap passed down a lane which ran past some open country where horses were being exercised. Lucy leaned forward to have a better look, and she could have sworn that one of the riders was Jasper. She was wrong, of course. Jasper had disappeared, and the galloping horse that this man was riding wasn't Rajah but a long-legged elegant bay. She heaved a sigh, and Miss May looked at her with some concern.

'I'm afraid you found today rather

tiring, Lucinda. Nevertheless you have made a good beginning. Your papa will be pleased.'

Lucy doubted that her father would be anything of the sort, for visiting the poor was women's work. She smiled and nodded at her governess, however, giving no inkling of the churning of her poor heart as she thought of the man she loved, who was now so far away . . .

Some days later there was a commotion in the hall, and Annie came flying up the stairs to the schoolroom to announce that their presence was requested in the morning-room by Lucy's father.

'Mr Ivory has come, Miss Lucinda,' she blurted. 'He's ever such a nice gentleman, Miss. So handsome and dressed in the height of fashion!'

Lucy was not impressed. 'Who is Mr Ivory? Surely he doesn't want to see me. Miss May and I were about to go out walking.'

'Oh, yes, Miss. The master was most

particular that he wanted you downstairs at once, and I think as you ought to go.'

'That will do, Annie, thank you.' Miss May dismissed Annie before she could say more and the girl bobbed a curtsey and left, leaving the door open.

'I believe we should obey Mr Ingram's summons, Lucinda. Come, let us go down.' Grumbling under her breath Lucy swept down the stairs with her governess bringing up the rear.

'Ah, there you are, Lucinda. May I introduce my cousin, Ronan Ivory?'

'How do you do, Mr Ivory.'

'How do you do?' the man who bent over to kiss her was tall and bewhiskered, and, as Annie had indicated, was smartly dressed. If Jasper had seen him he would have described Ivory as 'one of the nobs'. His gaze travelled over Lucy, causing her to blush. If anyone had looked at her like that in her former life she would have told him not to stare so rudely! The man ignored Miss May as being beneath his notice.

'Ronan and I are distant cousins,' Marcus Ingram commented. 'We'll be seeing much more of him in future, I hope, and I should like the two of you to be friends.'

Lucy didn't take to Ronan Ivory at all, but she did her best to be polite and was glad when her father excused her, saying that the two men had business matters to discuss.

'I don't see how we could possibly be friends,' she complained, when she and Miss May were out walking. 'I've heard that gentlemen have interests that are very different from ours, so what could we possibly have to talk about, other than the weather? You've already drummed into me that I mustn't discuss money, politics or religion at table, and no doubt the same applies in the drawing-room as well!'

Miss May hesitated. 'In your class, my dear, there really is no choice for a woman other than marriage and motherhood. Your dear father has explained that he wishes you to make a good marriage, and that is why I have been brought here to teach you how to behave in polite society. Believe me, an old maid is scorned by all! At least, that has been my experience.'

Her lips were set in a bitter line and Lucy realised that her friend was talking about herself. She hastened to say what she thought was the right thing.

'I'm sure you'll be married before me, Miss May. Why, haven't you noticed how often Mr Orton calls here to see us? It would be quite suitable if he should propose to you, for are you not a vicar's daughter? You know what is expected of a clergyman's wife! In time he will surely get a parish of his own and can then afford to marry.'

Miss May laughed grimly. 'You have quite the wrong idea. It is you who have caught Mr Orton's eye!'

Lucy opened her eyes wide. The thought had never occurred to her. She had naturally assumed that if there was anything more to his visits than encouraging them to perform good works it was Deborah May who had attracted his attention. Her mind then strayed to Cousin Ronan. She hoped that her father did not plan to marry her off to that gentleman, because she just wouldn't allow it!

Some days later, young Annie was thrilled when the housekeeper told her that she had been chosen to act as Miss Lucinda's personal maid. It was her ambition to become a ladies' maid and she saw this as the first step. Her duties involved pressing and mending Lucy's clothes and keeping her other belongings in good order.

For her part, Lucy was happy to have the little country girl to talk to. Miss May was pleasant company but she always insisted on doing 'the right thing' and Lucy always had to think twice before speaking her mind. For her part, Annie was not averse to a little gossip, no matter what Mrs Hyndman might say.

'What did you think of Mr Ivory,

Miss? Isn't he lovely?'

'I don't know about that, Annie. He strikes me as a rather cold person. Starchy.'

'I expect he'd be different when you got to know him, Miss. I mean, that's how married people are, like, easy together.'

'I have no wish to marry Mr Ivory,' Lucy said firmly, and was surprised by what Annie came out with next.

'Oh, but Cook said . . . ' the little maid broke off, biting her lip.

'And just what did Cook have to say?'

'Sorry, Miss, I spoke out of turn. I didn't mean nothing by it.'

'You'll tell me what she said if I have to shake you till your teeth rattle!' Lucy threatened, frowning horribly.

'Well, Mr Ivory used to come here a lot, you see, and what with the master having no sons, nor any children at all, till you came back, well, everybody said he was the master's heir. When the master dies, his cousin was supposed to come into all this, the estate and that.'

'And?'

'Well, you coming back means that Mr Ivory is out in the cold, see? And Cook reckons, well, she says if you was to marry Mr Ivory that would tie it up nicely. He wouldn't lose out after all.'

'I never heard anything so silly!' Lucy snapped. 'Kindly do not speak of this again!' It was a measure of Miss May's success as a teacher that Lucy was able to voice her thoughts in such a haughty manner. Not long ago she would have expressed herself in far more vulgar terms, and in much louder tones.

She had much to think about, however. While it was obvious that her parents were very wealthy people, she had given no thought as to where their possessions would go after they passed away. She had a vague idea that some big estates were entailed, meaning they had to be passed on to the nearest male relative, which would be a nephew or cousin if there was no son to inherit. It came as a shock that all this might be hers in due course.

And what if it were true? It would have come as a greater shock to Ronan Ivory to learn that all his expectations were to be dashed! And, if there was any substance to Cook's ramblings, perhaps he would see the solution to the problem as being marriage with his cousin, Lucinda. Did this meet with Marcus Ingram's approval? Was this the business that the two men had met to discuss?

If only she knew where to find Jasper! She would run to him at once to discuss this, but Jasper hadn't bothered to try to see her, or to send her any sort of message. He could write well enough, she knew, so why hadn't she heard from him?

6

'What did you say your name was?' Ned Jarvis had come into the yard and was bearing down on Jasper, who was cleaning out a stall.

'Gates, Sir. Jem Gates.' Trying to come up with an alias in a hurry, Jasper thought of the wrought iron gates at Briarwood Hall. Life on the road had taught him it was best not to give too much personal information in case it came back to haunt him at a later date. Petrel Lee was not the only member of their band to have been sentenced to transportation to Australia and the younger generation had learned their lesson well.

'I've been watching you, Gates.'

'Yes, Sir?' What now, Jasper wondered.

'You can ride as well as some, and better than most. That fool Pip

Merridew let his horse throw him at the races yesterday and broke his ankle. He won't be fit for work for weeks, if ever, and this leaves me without a jockey for this coming Saturday and I've several horses entered. I'm willing to put you up, if you feel so inclined.'

'Yes, Sir. Which horse will it be, begging your pardon, Sir?'

'King's Ransom, Gates, and bear in mind he's worth a king's ransom, and all. I saw how you handled him that first day you came, so I'm prepared to give you the chance. Ride him out with the string for the next few days, and we'll see how you get on.'

Several thoughts went through Jasper's mind as he turned back to his work. If he was given rides on a regular basis and, better yet, started to win, he would be given a share of the purse and could set money aside for the future. Despite the fact that the gypsies lived from day to day, he realised that if he hoped to win Lucy back he had to have something more to offer her.

Jasper wondered what Lucy was doing now. She had never responded to his note. He had waited for hours at the appointed place but she hadn't come. Something must have prevented her, that was plain to see.

One day after that he had mounted Rajah and ridden over to the Hall and had actually caught a glimpse of her, although it had taken him a moment to recognise her, all decked out in her new finery. He hadn't been able to approach her, though, because there was another woman with her. Could it be her mother? At that distance it was impossible to tell the age of the person walking sedately at Lucy's side.

He was not prepared to give up so easily. He would return again and again, if necessary, until he could catch her on her own. If that didn't work out, he could send another note, or even march up to the door and demand to see her.

He wouldn't expect her to come away with him just yet, of course. She needed more time to adjust to her new life and to come to a decision about her future. He just wanted to make sure she was all right.

* * *

Lucy was in bed with a headache. One of the more useful lessons she had learned from Miss May was that a lady could always get out of an unpleasant situation by pleading to have a pounding head.

'I'll pull the curtains to keep the light out, Miss Lucy. You don't want the sun shining in your eyes. If you don't feel like coming down for luncheon, I'll bring you up a tray.'

'Thank you, Annie.' Lucy spoke faintly and moved her legs restlessly. Miss May had placed a cold cloth on her head and dabbed lavender water on her wrists and tiptoed out. No doubt she was thankful to have some time to herself.

Left alone, Lucy sank back on her

pillows with a sigh. There was nothing wrong with her head at all, but she needed time to think. Yesterday she had gone up to the old nurseries and had looked around, vainly trying to conjure up some old memories, for it was here that she had spent the first months of her life. Of course, she could remember nothing that far back; nobody could.

There must have been a nanny, who had come to take charge of her after the monthly nurse had left, and at least one nursemaid. That was Polly somebody, the girl who had taken her eyes off her long enough for Mariah to swoop down and snatch her up. Lucy wished she could speak to these women, to ask them what had happened when she was found to be missing.

Had the nanny been dismissed in disgrace as well, or simply let go when it became evident that the baby wasn't coming back, and she was no longer needed? How long had it been before Sophia Ingram had given up hope and retired to her couch to lead the life of an invalid?

Too upset to go to sleep, Lucy got up and went to the window. Her room was at the front of the house and afforded a view of the main gates, and part of the lodge beyond them. She could just make out the figure of a man, standing beside a horse, apparently not planning to come inside. It was impossible to tell who he was, but the horse seemed familiar. Rajah! And where Rajah was, Jasper could not be far behind.

With a robe over her nightgown, and an all-enveloping shawl over that, she rushed down the stairs in her bare feet and flew across the immaculate lawns, only to come to a sudden halt, half blinded by tears of disappointment when she realised that Jasper had gone.

'Lucinda! What on earth are you doing, out here half dressed? Anyone could have seen you. Just suppose if Mr Ivory had been here!'

'There was a horseman, Miss May. I thought . . . ' But Miss May was never to know what that thought was, because Lucy bit back the words in time. It would never do to let her governess know about Jasper. Fortunately the other woman misunderstood.

'I'm delighted to know that you are so eager to see Mr Ivory, Lucinda, but I urge you to hide your feelings for him. Gentlemen do not care for girls who wear their heart on their sleeves, and he would certainly not approve your lack of decorum! If you are to marry into your proper class you must learn to behave as a lady should! Now, I suggest you go upstairs at once and dress yourself, for if your headache has quite gone we can settle down to our lessons.'

'Yes, Miss May.' Lucy trudged back to the house, her mind in a whirl. Where had Jasper sprung from? She longed to see her people again. Was Ezra still alive? Was Mariah worrying about her? She missed them all, even the grumpy Lark. She longed to be walking the country lanes once more, to be clasped in Jasper's arms, to sleep in her own caravan under star-studded skies. Her people! But the Ingrams were her family now, and she was learning to lead a very different like.

Deborah May sought out Annie and interrogated her crossly.

'I've just found Miss Lucinda outside, dressed in her night clothes. Whatever possessed her to do such a thing?'

Annie frowned. 'I don't know, Miss May, I don't really. I laid out her clothes this morning, same as usual, not that I expected her to put them on, seeing as she was so poorly, like. Mebbe she was sleep walking and didn't know what she was doing?'

'I hardly think so, Annie. By what she told me I have the idea that she thought she caught a glimpse of Mr Ivory from the window and ran out to greet him.'

'Oh, no, Miss, not in her night clothes! And Mr Ivory isn't expected today, is he? No, I'm sure it couldn't be that.'

'Well, she certainly ran out to meet

somebody, and that must be important for her to behave in so disgraceful a fashion. Do you know anything about it?'

'Oh, no, Miss!'

Miss May went away, not at all satisfied. Annie went straight to Cook.

'Didn't you tell me some gypsy lad came to the door a while back, asking for Miss Lucinda?'

Cook reached for a wooden spoon and squinted at Annie. The kitchen was full of steam and she was feeling frazzled.

'Yes, he did, and Mrs Hyndman was none too pleased about it, neither. Gave me a note for the miss, he did, and soon as the woman got her hands on it, straight into the fire it went. That's the last we'll hear from him, no doubt.'

'That was cruel, Cook. Don't you think we should let Miss Lucy know?'

'I do not! What if the master got to hear about it, eh? It was one of them blessed gypsies as stole that baby away, and nearly drove the poor mistress out of her mind. To this day she's not normal, never mind as Miss Lucinda is back where she belongs.' She turned back to the pot she was stirring, making it plain that the subject was closed.

Annie scooted as fast as her legs would carry her. She found Lucy still dressed in her nighclothes and shawl.

'I've come to help you dress, Miss Lucy,' she said firmly. 'And just look at your poor feet, cold as ice, I'll be bound.'

Lucy sighed but allowed Annie to help her with her corset. 'Don't lace me too tight, Annie. It makes me feel like I'm in prison. I don't know what's so important about having an eighteen inch waist, anyway. If men had to wear corsets the fashion wouldn't last long!'

'No, Miss.'

'Do you like working in this house, Annie? Doesn't it bother you to work day and night, with only one afternoon a week for yourself? Don't you long to be free?'

'What's free, Miss? I'm the oldest of

eleven children. Before I come here I lived in a tiny cottage with all of us squeezed in, and not enough food to go round. Here I've got me own room and three meals a day. What more could I want?'

Lucy sighed. She certainly wanted more, and it seemed as if she wasn't going to get it.

7

Lucy was having a reading lesson. She could already read to some extent, having attended a village school from time to time, but words of more than one syllable were beyond her.

'It is generally thought that a gentlewoman does not need much education,' Miss May said primly, 'and gentlemen prefer that. It would never do for a wife to be more knowledgeable than her husband! As long as she can run her household well, and converse on many subjects, although nothing controversial, she will do very well. However, one can derive much pleasure from reading novels and that is why it would be well for you to improve your standard a little.'

Because of Lucy's age, Miss May decided against using the primers which were languishing on the schoolroom shelves, all of 'the cat sat on the mat' variety. Instead, she provided some light novels from the penny lending library.

'Ooh, I like the sound of that,' Annie said, gazing at a copy of Her Lost Love. 'Can I have it after you, Miss?'

This, more than anything else, spurred Lucy to improve, for she didn't want her maid to outdo her. In this way, several weeks went by pleasantly.

One morning she was in the part of the grounds where the head gardener grew flowers for cutting. Miss May had been teaching her the correct method of arranging flowers, which Lucy found interesting if a little pointless.

She was surprised when the Reverend Clement Orton came around the side of the house and halted in front of her, holding his large hat in both hands.

'Good morning, Miss Ingram.'

'Good morning, Mr Orton. Have you come about the jumble sale? I believe that Miss May has everything ready for you. Shall I go and fetch her?'

'Er, no. It is you to whom I wish to speak.'

Lucy wondered why the gentry had to speak in such a convoluted manner, but she smiled gently and waited for him to go on. Stammering and stuttering, he finally managed to get the words out.

'I have conceived a great admiration for you, Miss Ingram, and I beg you will do me the honour of consenting to become my wife.'

'Oh, I couldn't possibly!' Lucy cried, realising as soon as the words were out of her mouth that this was hurtful. The memory of the book she had just finished reading came to her rescue, and she quoted the heroine, Fabiola Marchmont. 'I mean, this is so sudden, Mr Orton! And what will my papa say?' She closed her mouth, feeling foolish.

Fabiola's suitor had gone away at once, with his stiff upper lip very much in evidence. Fabiola had gone through a number of unsuitable men before she finally met her true love and accepted his kiss while moonlight filtered down through the branches of the willow tree under which they were standing.

Mr Orton had obviously had little practice in dealing with the heroines of popular fiction, for he nodded happily as if Lucy had said exactly the right thing.

'Of course, Miss Ingram. I do understand. It is quite proper for a modest young lady such as yourself to say no at first, and of course I shall seek your papa's permission at the earliest opportunity.'

'My father is away from home just now,' Lucy muttered, 'and I'm not sure that he wishes me to marry yet awhile. Miss May says I have much to learn before that time. The running of a household and so on,' she continued vaguely.

'It must be a long engagement, of course,' he agreed. 'I cannot marry until I have a parish of my own. Nevertheless, it will be good to have the matter settled. I bid you good day.'

He walked off jauntily, leaving Lucy reeling. What on earth had she done? She had tried to refuse his very unromantic proposal, but somehow he had been left with the idea that she was not averse to the idea. She rushed off to find her governess, earning a rebuke for dashing about in an unladylike manner, showing her ankles in the process.

'I've had a proposal,' she groaned. 'From Mr Orton!' Did she imagine it, or did a shadow pass over Miss May's face? Lucy felt, not for the first time, that life could be very unfair. It looked as if Deborah May fancied the curate, who hardly noticed her existence, while he wanted to marry Lucy, who wouldn't give him the time of day!

'And what was your response?'

'That's just it, Miss May! I thought I was turning him down, but it all went wrong and now he's going to speak to Papa and ask for my hand!'

'I doubt if Mr Ingram would agree, my dear. I fancy he has other plans for you. You must go to your papa when he returns home and explain what has happened. He will refuse Mr Orton on your behalf, and you will have nothing more to worry about.'

Lucy wasn't so sure. One way and another they spent a lot of time at the church, and she could hardly avoid meeting Mr Orton there. She didn't want to spend the rest of her life with his reproachful eyes on her. Perhaps Papa could get the man transferred to another parish or something? Miss May didn't think so.

'But a young woman in your position will have to get used to such proposals. It may not have occurred to you, but you are now a wealthy heiress, and an eligible marriage prospect among the gentlemen of the county.'

Lucy pulled a wry face. Such a notion was new to her, and she wasn't at all sure that she liked it.

★　★　★

Full of himself, Clement Orton went straight to the vicar, whom he found in his study, pouring over an unfinished sermon. Arthur Brown let his subordinate wait for a full minute before he looked up, frowning.

'And where do you think you've been, Orton?'

'Up to the Hall, Vicar.'

'Despite the fact that three members of the flower guild waited for you for over half an hour? What was so important that you couldn't even send word to let them know you weren't coming? Surely not the jumble!'

Orton reddened. 'I wanted to make my intentions plain to a certain lady, Vicar. Oh, I know I have no hope of marrying yet, but I shall be in a position to take a wife some day and I wished to propose before someone else does.'

'It's Miss Deborah May, of course. Well, I approve, Orton! A very pleasant woman as far as I can tell. Past the first flush of youth, of course, but none the worse for that, and as a clergyman's daughter she'll be well aware of what is expected as helpmate in the parish.'

'Oh, it's not Miss May. No, it's Miss Lucinda Ingram on whom my heart is set.'

The vicar's jaw dropped. 'Are you mad, Orton? She's Marcus Ingram's heiress. He'd never permit her to marry a poor clergyman and there are other things to be taken into consideration as well.'

'I don't see why not. The fact that she has been brought up by gypsies might make her unsuitable in the eyes of the county. I doubt if any of the nobility would consider taking her into their families for a start!'

'That's precisely what I mean, Orton. What about the parishioners? If you ever aspire to your own parish you'd better think again. Can you imagine that girl presiding over the tea table at the church fete?'

'The cottage people speak highly of her and gladly welcome her into their homes. Why should it be different anywhere else?'

The vicar heaved a loud sigh. 'Are you really such a fool? Of course they like her in the village. She's a novelty, man. Also, she's Marcus Ingram's daughter, and that counts for something. As a clergyman's wife she would be resented. What sort of example would she be able to set? When she is trying to offer guidance, they'd remember her gypsy life. Traipsing around England selling clothes pegs! Telling fortunes, which is nothing but superstition! Stealing chickens for the pot, I daresay. And who knows what other immoral behaviour she may have participated in?

'Have you ever seen a gypsy wedding? I'm told that the couple hold hands and jump over a broomstick to cement their union, and they never see the inside of a church. That is not Holy wedlock, Orton! Why, for all you know she may have taken part in such a union, possibly with the young gypsy lad who delivered her here to my door.' He paused, out of breath.

A stubborn look crossed Clement Orton's face. 'I've listened carefully to all you've said, Vicar, and I thank you for the advice, which no doubt is kindly meant. However, I intend to proceed. The young woman herself has not turned me down, and that being the case I shall approach Mr Ingram as soon as he returns home. And if it is true that we should not be accepted in England despite the fact that her kidnapping and subsequent life was not her fault — then I shall apply to go to the mission field. No doubt the heathen will be more charitable.'

The vicar sniffed loudly and fumbled for his handkerchief. 'Then on your head be it. Do not come to me when everything falls apart.'

The King's Arms was a public house, situated on the road leading from Briarwood to Ned Jarvis's racing stable. The patrons included both the men from the village and Jarvis's stablemen and jockeys. Nobody thought anything of Jasper turning up there on a Saturday night with his work mates but he had an ulterior motive for going. He hoped to get news of the Hall, and of course of Lucy.

The first few times there was no mention of her, and he woke up the next morning with a throbbing head as a result of drinking too much ale. On one wet night, things were different. Outside the rain was teeming down, and the tap room was filled with steam as men sat as close to the fire as possible in an attempt to dry off their wet clothes. Jasper pricked up his ears when he heard Lucy's name.

'Ay, a right nice young gal, for all she'd been brought up by them gyppos as stole her,' one ancient fellow mumbled. 'Comes to my daughter's cottage, she does, and brings little bits of leftovers from up the Hall. Don't suppose she'll be around much longer, though. They'll have her married off in two shakes of a lamb's tail, you see if they don't.'

Jasper edged closer to the speaker and his crony. 'Be that Miss Lucinda you be talking about?' he asked. They looked at him with the suspicion that is always meted out to strangers in country places.

'What's it to you, lad?'

'I've seen her out walking, with another lady, when I was just passing by. I thought she was a pretty one, that's all.'

'Ah! Looking's all you'll get to do, my lad! She's a rich man's daughter, she is. I daresay her dad'll have some fine gentleman in mind for her to wed. Someone from their own class, like.'

'So she's not betrothed yet, then?'

'Not so far as I know, but it may not be long. There's two gentlemen after her already, that's what I heard.'

'You didn't tell me that, Sid,' his friend said.

'No, well, there's nothing official that I knows of, but our Fanny, her as works at the vicarage, she heard the vicar and that Mr Orton having a right set-to. Seems the curate proposed to Miss Lucinda and thinks he's in with a chance. Vicar, though, he says 'you great fool, who'd have you?' but Mr Orton says he's going to speak to Mr Ingram anyhow. Not that he'll get anywhere, and him as poor as a church mouse.'

'And who's the other one, then?' Jasper said carelessly.

'Ah! Now that's a different story. Mr Ronan Ivory, that's who.'

'Who's Ronan Ivory when he's at home?'

'Mr Ingram's cousin. The Ingrams never had no children, apart from Miss Lucinda, and when she disappeared and they didn't know if she was alive or dead, then twas Mr Ivory who was named heir to the estate. Now she's come back and Ivory's nose is out of joint, good and proper.'

The old man's friend took up the tale. 'And now he's sniffing around Miss Lucinda, thinking to put that right by marrying her, I s'pose. When a woman marries all her property goes to her husband. I should know, because when my Bess come to me she brought three sheep and a copper kettle by way of a dowry, see?'

Jasper felt a pang at the thought of his lovely Lucy being married off for the sake of the money she stood to inherit, spending the rest of her life tied up in a loveless marriage while her husband squandered the lot. 'It don't seem natural to me,' he said at last, but his two companions disagreed.

'Tis the way of the world, lad. Great landowners have always arranged marriages for their children. And what does a woman know about managing an estate such as Briarwood? Stands to reason Ingram would want her yoked to a steady fellow, eh?'

'If he is a steady fellow!' his friend sneered.

Jasper was alarmed. 'What are you saying, mister? Is there something wrong with this Ivory chap?'

'None of your business if you know what's good for you, and none of ours, neither!'

The two old men changed the subject then, and refused to be drawn again. Jasper knew he had to find out more about Ronan Ivory. Luckily a crippled groom at the stables had plenty to say when asked if he had ever heard of the man.

'Ronan Ivory! May he rot in hell! I used to ride his horses, didn't I? Then when I got thrown and broke both legs he threw me out on my ear without a penny piece in compensation, never mind all the races I'd won for him in my time. He made a mint of money out of me, so he did. Lucky for me I had somewhere to go. My sister took me in till I got back on my feet, but I'll never ride again, and she couldn't keep me there forever. If it wasn't for Mr Jarvis giving me this job I'd be in the workhouse now.' He spat into the straw, wiping his mouth with the back of his hand.

'Are any of his horses here now?' Jasper knew that many owners sent their animals to Ned Jarvis to be trained.

'What horses? He may own one or two for hunting, or getting about the country, but race horses? Nah! Couldn't afford Jarvis's fees. The word is our Mr Ivory is close to bankrupt. He owes money all around the country on account of he likes to gamble.'

Jasper saw it all. Ivory was one of those profligate men who inherited money from his family and proceeded to squander it until there was nothing left.

What a shock it must have been when Lucy turned up again. Now she was to be the sacrificial lamb so he could reclaim his fortune. Jasper refused to believe that Lucy could fall in love with such a man, but might Ivory be able to convince her that he was in love with her?

Jasper reflected grimly that marriage to Lucy would enable Ivory to continue with his wasteful lifestyle, if only for as long as it took him to run through that inheritance too. After that, what would happen to her? Jasper realised that the wedding must be prevented at all costs, but what could he do?

He had encouraged Lucy to return to the Ingrams, at least until she could decide whether she wanted to go or stay, but what did he have to offer her if she came back to him?

His savings had not grown as fast as he'd hoped. The few coins in the money belt he wore around his waist were not enough to buy a horse, let alone the trappings of the genteel lifestyle she was now enjoying. He had won several races but although the owners showered praise on him they were less ready to share the winnings with him.

Most were reluctant to loosen their purse strings even when the guineas he had won for them represented more than an ordinary working man would earn in ten years. It seemed that old lame Foster knew what he was talking about.

Tossing and turning in his narrow bed at night, Jasper came to a decision. He must go to the Hall and try once again to speak to Lucy. If he found that she still loved him, he would try to convince her to come away with him while there was still time, or at least to remain single until he could make enough money to return for her. How he would do that was still a mystery, but if all else failed he would go in search of his people and see if he could borrow money from them.

8

Lucy was walking sedately through the grounds of Briarwood Hall. If a practitioner of the new art of photography had been present to record the scene, this would have been the end product, in sepia tones on a cardboard backing.

Lucy was wearing a new dress of many layers, buttoned up to the neck despite the heat of the day. Ladies never perspired, they 'glowed', but she was coming close to that state and wondered what could be so disgraceful about a natural function. She carried a parasol to keep the sun's rays off her face; a lady must always have a pale complexion. Miss May despaired of Lucy's sun-browned skin and had suggested that if the tan didn't fade over the winter, they would have to use arsenic to do the job.

'Only cottage women let the weather affect them,' she had said, 'and even then they wear sunbonnets when they go into the fields at harvest time.' She might have added gypsies to that class of woman, but a lady was supposed to keep negative opinions to herself.

Ronan Ivory was walking beside Lucy. He had tempered his stride to fall in with her slower gait. Hampered by her skirts she could not go any faster, and of course a lady never travelled in haste!

Miss May, acting as chaperone, walking a few paces behind the couple, longed to go inside and put her feet up, with a cool glass of raspberry vinegar in her hand. The procession reached the boundary fence and turned to go back the way they had come.

'I always enjoyed coming here as a boy,' Ivory said. 'I can remember when you were born, you know.'

'Do you?' Lucy smiled up at him, feeling Miss May's eyes on her.

'Oh, yes. I was seven years old and

had just completed my first term at boarding school. I could not go home because one of my sisters was quarantined with some childhood disease so I was sent here instead. I was told that I had to be very quiet in the house because Cousin Sophia wasn't very well but there was a baby upstairs which cried a lot and the maids laughed at me when I asked why the creature wasn't made to keep quiet as well.'

Lucy smiled again. She wondered what this was leading up to.

'So you see there has been a connection between us almost since the day you were born,' he went on.

'I see.' Lucy was finding that this little expression was quite useful when a meaningless response was called for. Of course there was a connection, that of a blood tie between them. She wondered how long it had been before it had occurred to Ronan Ivory that with her apparently gone for good, and that if the Ingrams were not blessed with other children, then he might inherit Briarwood.

'You are thinking that we have so much time to make up,' he said now. 'I mean to come here much more often so we can get to know each other properly.'

Lucy squirmed. She wanted to nip this in the bud, as Mariah was fond of saying.

'That would be lovely,' she lied. 'Of course, I may not be here much longer.'

His eyebrows shot up. 'How so?'

She smiled sweetly. 'I have had a proposal of marriage, from the Reverend Clement Orton. He means to speak to my Papa, you know.'

Ivory's expression darkened. For a moment he looked quite angry. 'And have you accepted him?'

'Oh, no. That would not be proper at all. I must wait and see what Papa says.' She was rather proud of herself for saying this. She hoped it would have a two-fold result. It would prevent Ivory from declaring himself in the near future, and if he went to Marcus

Ingram to complain, that would effectively spoil Mr Orton's chances as well. If as she suspected her father meant to encourage Cousin Ronan he would send the curate away without further ado.

Out of the corner of her eye, Miss May noticed a fellow standing in the wood, who seemed to be watching them. If he was a wood cutter he was certainly not doing his job, but if he was a stranger, what was he doing there? She made up her mind to report this to Mr Ingram.

On the other side of the boundary wall, Jasper drew back behind a mighty oak tree, almost sure that the woman had noticed him. He had been careless there, but the sight of his Lucy strolling along with that gentleman at her elbow had thrown him into a rage, sure that it was Ronan Ivory.

His first impulse was to leap over the wall, run after the couple and flatten the fellow with one well-aimed punch. Then he could talk to Lucy and find out what was going on. With a great effort he held himself in check. The companion or whatever she was, would scream for help and servants would come running.

Ivory, when he recovered, would lay charges against Jasper, and with Marcus Ingram being a magistrate the case wouldn't even come to court. He would be delivered to the peelers and find himself in gaol before you could say knife!

He must come back after dark and try to see Lucy then. Perhaps he could bribe one of the servants to get a message to her. Or, wait — hadn't he seen a coachman at the tavern, a bow-legged man who worked at Briarwood Hall? Perhaps he could strike up a conversation with this chap, get him drunk and wheedle useful information out of him?

Ronan Ivory's mind was working furiously. He had suppressed his anger with difficulty while accompanying Lucinda and Miss May back to the house, and was now pacing up and down in the room allotted to him. Marcus Ingram had told him that he favoured a marriage between him and Lucinda but had stressed that she was not to be forced into wedlock against her will.

'The poor girl has suffered enough, Ronan. I want to ensure that her future will be a happy one, with the man of her choice. I cannot deny that I hope she will choose you; there is more than one wrong to be righted here.'

'Time and patience!' Ivory muttered now, through gritted teeth. If only that were all! A thousand curses on that measly curate! He could of course demand to see Cousin Marcus as soon as he arrived home, getting in first before the curate had the chance of a hearing. He was fairly sure that Marcus would offer a firm refusal, even without his own intervention, but he could not afford to take that chance.

Was Lucinda in love with the little curate? It wouldn't be the first time that some heiress had decided to disobey her parents and elope with the man of her choice. Once the wedding had taken place and the marriage consummated there would be no turning back. No, there was only one thing for it. He must get to this Reverend Orton and warn him off.

The door of the vicarage was opened by Fanny, whose first impulse was to shut it in his face. Having seen his lowering expression she could tell that trouble was looming and she felt a certain protectiveness towards the reverend gentlemen she served.

'I don't think they're at home, Sir,' she began. Actually both men were at their dinner, but this wasn't a lie. In polite circles 'not at home' could also mean the householder was not receiving visitors, a widely accepted practice.

As she told her friends later, a true gentleman would have offered his card, whereupon she would have taken it through to the vicar and let him make the decision as to whether the visitor was to be admitted. Ronan Ivory did not give her the chance, but pushed past her in a rude manner and burst into the dining-room, where the two clergymen looked up from the table in surprise.

'Ronan Ivory!' he snapped. 'And you are?'

The vicar looked him up and down with icy disdain. 'I am the Reverend Arthur Brown, and this is my assistant, Clement Orton. Is there some emergency that you see fit to interrupt us when we are dining?'

Ivory ignored him. Turning to Orton he looked him straight in the eye and began the dressing down he had come to deliver.

'I understand that you've had the audacity to propose marriage to my cousin, Miss Ingram!'

'I did invite her to join me in that honourable estate, yes.' As Lucy had done, the vicar felt some irritation at Orton's awkward words, yet he conceded that the man didn't deserve this drubbing. He decided he'd better remain on the scene in case the pair came to blows and poor Orton needed assistance.

'And has my cousin accepted your proposal?'

'I cannot see that it is any of your business, Sir; however, Miss Lucinda has very properly declined to give me her answer until we learn what her father has to say on the matter. I am confident that if he looks with favour on my suit Miss Lucinda will then agree to become my wife.'

'Over my dead body!' Ivory shouted. 'I have come to state — no, to demand — that you must leave my cousin alone, or it will be the worse for you!'

Clement Orton might be just a poor curate in a country parish, but he was no coward. He got up from the table and, very much on his dignity, stared Ivory down.

'As I remarked before, the decision rests with Miss Lucinda and her father, and on that account there is nothing

114

more to be said. Good evening to you, Sir.' He wiped his mouth on his napkin and walked out of the room.

The vicar's nostrils flared. If Ivory had known the man for very long he would have recognised the fact that Arthur Brown was on the verge of losing his temper.

'I suppose this means that you have hopes of Miss Ingram yourself,' he said coldly. 'I can think of no other reason for you to have forced your way in here and harangued my curate, before we have even finished our meal. Certainly this is no way for a gentleman to behave, and I must tell you that my housekeeper was quite correct in stating that we are not at home to such as you. Unless you have something to add, I suggest you be on your way.'

He picked up his spoon, leaving Ivory speechless and at a loss. He turned on his heel and stormed out.

'Good riddance to bad rubbish!' Fanny grumbled as she slammed the door behind him. Mr Orton was foolish, of course, as she would have pointed out to him had she dared. That Miss Lucinda was an heiress. Some day she would own Marcus Ingram's wealth and the whole Briarwood estate, or at least, the man she married would have it. Mr Orton could not aspire to all that, and neither would Miss Lucinda leave all that and go to live with him in some little parish in the middle of nowhere.

It was obvious of course why this Ivory person wanted Mr Orton to be warned off. He wanted Miss Lucinda for himself, and he didn't want any other man queering his pitch. She rubbed her hands in glee. All this was something to tell her cronies. What luck to be right on the spot when Mr Ronan Ivory came calling!

Ronan Ivory mounted his horse in a foul mood. He jerked the poor creature's mouth around and dug his heels into its flank with more force than necessary. Damn that Orton, and damn Lucinda! He would have given a lot to know what answer she would have given had she known the man would receive a favourable response from her father!

As it was, Ivory would have liked to get hold of the minx and shake her until her teeth rattled and force her to agree to marry him. But that would not do. Although she had been brought up among the gypsies she was a lady by birth, and she could not be dealt with as if she was some little cottage drab, to be taken and discarded.

For a long moment he considered doing just that; once she was ruined she would be thankful for any decent man to take her on, but there was Marcus Ingram to be considered. As a magistrate he was upright in his beliefs and he might well order his servants to give Ivory the whipping he deserved.

Therefore, Ivory had to strive to remain patient, which was far from easy. He thought ruefully of the pile of dunning letters that awaited payment. Not just the bills from his tailor and wine merchant — no gentleman ever paid those on time — but the more worrisome gambling debts which by now had mounted into thousands of pounds. If those weren't paid soon, the bailiffs would move in. he'd lose his own family estate and he'd be disgraced, and his sisters left homeless. Unthinkable!

Even if he married Lucinda, it might be quite some time before he inherited Briarwood. Marcus Ingram was a comparatively young man and might go on for many years yet. He could probably be persuaded to settle a goodly sum on his daughter in the meantime, but would that be enough?

It was no longer possible for him to borrow from friends. They had shelled out too much for him already and it had reached the point where they were 'not at home' when he called. Something had to be done, and done soon.

9

'He's a right cad, that one!' Marcus Ingram's coachman was sunk in gloom, staring into his pint pot as if to find the solution to the mysteries of the universe in the bottom.

'Ready for another?' Jasper picked up the tankard and had it refilled at the counter. The coachman appeared to have an infinite capacity for ale, having the proverbial hollow leg. So far the drink hadn't loosened his tongue but it seemed at last as if he might be ready to talk. Perhaps this last pint would do it.

'Not popular with the staff then, is he, this Ronan Ivory?'

'Popular! Popular as a weasel, him.'

'A bit slow with the tips, is he?'

'Slow! He never gives nothing to nobody. Not that many tips comes my way, for I never serve visitors, but most guests gives something to the house-maid what does their room, or sends something down as a compliment to the cook for their good dinners. No, he's a skinflint, is Ivory.'

'But you say you have nothing to do with him anyway, so why the hard feelings?'

The man grunted. 'Tried to punch the lights out of me, didn't he?'

'What?'

'You heard what I said. Came at me, hammer and tongs, 'cause I wouldn't do what he wanted. I was at the stable, see, harnessing up the horses to take the master to town, when this Ivory happens by. 'Give my horse a good rub down, my man,' he says, all uppity like. I'm sorry, Sir, I says, that ain't my job. You'll need to ask one of the grooms. That's when he hit me, and more than once, too. 'Take that for your insolence my man,' he says. For two pins I'd have let him have a good one back, but for I've my living to earn. He's the master's cousin and Mr Ingram don't stand no nonsense, see?'

Jasper saw. 'Aye, it's a hard world,' he grunted. 'How would you like to get back at Ivory?'

'Wassat? How?'

'I need help to get a message to Miss Lucy. I've got to get her out of there before Ivory gets her in his clutches. He wants to marry her, see?'

The man peered at him suspiciously. 'What's it to you, then?'

'She's my girl. I love her, and I mean to marry her myself.'

The coachman let out a great guffaw. 'Garn, you're mazed in the head! Marry Miss Lucinda? A simple working chap like you, marrying into the gentry?'

'It's true enough,' Jasper said with dignity. 'By hook or by crook I have to get into that house and you're the man to help me.'

The coachman shambled to his feet. 'I'll have no part of it. How do I know you don't mean to get inside to rob them blind? I don't want to spend the rest of my born days breaking up rocks in the penitentiary!' He stumbled out of the tavern, leaving a cursing Jasper behind. All that ale money down the drain, and no further ahead! What was worse, the man might go to warn Marcus Ingram, or at least be overheard talking about his encounter in the tavern.

Jasper made his way back to Jarvis's as fast as possible. That way, if they came looking for him, he could not be identified as the possible burglar. Another day gone by, and he was no nearer to seeing Lucy.

He could go back to the Hall and keep watch from the woods in the hope of seeing her out walking, but how could he get her alone? She always had that dowdy-looking woman with her; some kind of servant, he supposed. Could she be bribed, or was she paid to keep Lucy from having any contact with the gypsies? He dared not take the chance of approaching her. He would have to think of something else.

'I thought I should warn you, Cousin Marcus.'

'About what?' Marcus Ingram passed a box of cigars to Ivory, who took one and studied it carefully before replying.

'The curate, name of Orton, I believe.'

'What about him?'

'He dares to think that he would make a suitable husband for Lucinda. In fact, I believe that he has already proposed to her.'

'Oh? And how did she deal with that?'

'As she told me herself, she merely referred him to you.'

'Then where is the problem, Ronan? When he arrives I shall simply tell him that marriage with my daughter is out of the question.'

Ivory hesitated. 'I fear there is danger of her running off with him, Cousin Marcus. She would not be the first flighty young miss to elope, only to regret it for the rest of her life.'

Ingram looked at his young cousin through narrowed eyes. He wasn't sure where this was leading, but he meant to get to the bottom of it, and quickly.

'You did right in coming to me, Ronan. Now, if you'll excuse me, I'm a busy man.'

Ivory found himself outside the study door, fuming. Had he overplayed his hand? After a moment's thought, Marcus Ingram crossed the room and jerked the bell pull. When the maid arrived he barked out an order without looking at her.

'Find Miss Lucinda at once and tell her I need to see her. At once, girl! Don't stand there gaping!'

'Yes, Sir!' The girl scuttled off to find Annie.

'Seems in a right tizzy. I don't know what Miss Lucinda's done, but she's to get down there quick, sharp!'

'All right, Mary. I'll see that she gets the message at once.'

When Lucy arrived at the study,

wondering why she'd been summoned, she found her father standing at the window, placidly smoking his cigar.

'Ah, Lucinda, my dear. Please sit down.'

Lucy subsided on to a high-backed chair, carefully arranging her skirts around her. 'You wished to see me, Papa?' She realised at once what a silly question this was; why else would he have sent for her? But she couldn't just sit there like a stuffed dummy, and Miss May was valiantly trying to teach her the art of polite conversation.

'I shall come to the point, Lucinda. I believe that a certain clergyman had made a proposal of marriage to you?'

'Oh, so he's been to see you, then?'

'Not yet, as it happens, but someone else has brought this to my attention.'

'Miss May, I suppose.'

'It was not, as a matter of fact.'

Lucy said nothing, thinking that Annie must have said something.

'So, kindly tell me how you reacted to this proposal?'

'I told Mr Orton that he must speak to you, Papa.'

'Quite right and proper, but what are your feelings for the man?'

'I do not care for him at all, Papa, but his proposal was so unexpected that I didn't know what to say. I felt that you could deal with it so much better than I.' Once again Lucy was proud of herself. She had a quick memory, and that stilted little speech was a direct quotation from the current novel. There was a time when she might have said 'seeing him off with a flea in his ear'. She smiled.

Her father seemed pleased with her. 'Very well, my dear, you can trust me to deal with the fellow. You may go now, back to your lessons.' Lucy went, closing the door quietly behind her.

Lucy and Miss May had walked down to the church, their arms full of late blooming flowers from the gardens of Briarwood Hall. Having spent some time with a crippled old cottager on the anniversary of his wife's death, Miss

May was now, at his request, going to place flowers on the grave as he was unable to go there himself.

'Some of them chrysanths will do a treat, if you can spare 'em, Miss. She liked a nice chrysanth, did my Mary.' His tiny garden plot, which had been ablaze with flowers in his wife's day, was now neglected and overgrown with weeds, for he could no longer do the work himself and his daughter, who lived next door, was too busy with her large brood of children to assist.

'You go on into the church and arrange the rest of the flowers, Lucinda,' Miss May instructed. 'I shall be with you shortly.'

Lucy was glad to have a few minutes to herself, but felt embarrassed and none too pleased when she heard quick footsteps on the stone floor and looked up from her work to find Mr Orton approaching. Where was Miss May when she was needed?

After a great deal of throat clearing, the curate blurted out something about wanting to speak to her. Seeing that there was no way to escape, Lucy managed a weak smile and waited.

'It seems that I must withdraw my offer of marriage, Miss Ingram,' he began. 'Your father has indicated that he has other plans for you, and that I must respect. I must say however that I felt it quite unnecessary for your cousin to come to the vicarage and threaten me as he did.'

'My cousin! Do you mean Mr Ivory?'

'Exactly. I cannot believe that your father sent him as an emissary, for at that time I had yet to announce my intentions to Mr Ingram.'

Rage boiled up inside Lucy. Ronan Ivory had no right to take it upon himself to speak to the little curate as he had. While she would never in a thousand years have agreed to marry Clement Orton it was good of him to have proposed to her and he didn't deserve to be treated so badly.

It was one thing for her father to deliver a firm refusal — that was what fathers were for — but quite another for their cousin to interfere. Looking at Mr Orton's woebegone face she cast aside the polite language of society, so painfully learned, and decided to speak from the heart. Miss May would not approve, but that lady was out of earshot. Lucy took a deep breath.

'I'm sorry that you have been insulted by my cousin, Mr Orton. He had no right to speak. But I'm afraid I should not be a suitable wife for you at all. You need someone who is in tune with your lifestyle, somebody who had been brought up in the Church of England, someone your parishioners will accept as one of their own. Someone like Miss May, for instance.'

'Miss May?' he said vaguely. 'Do I know her?'

'Yes, of course you do! Miss Deborah May, my governess. She's a clergyman's daughter, you know, and until he died she kept house for her widowed father and helped him with social work in the parish. Yes, Miss May would suit you very well. Mr Orton, you should give it some thought.'

Those remarks left the curate speech-less, as well they might. It wasn't every spurned suitor who was given the name of a replacement and told to get on with it!

Miss May walked in at that moment and was puzzled when the curate turned to look at her with some speculation. Feeling that she had gone too far, Lucy turned to her governess and broke into a long explanation of how she had arranged the flowers, but that some adjustment might be needed in the altar vases. Miss May went to look at them and after a moment Mr Orton turned on his heel and left. Lucy heaved a sigh of relief.

Life suddenly became very busy, for the autumn season was about to begin, and Lucy was to be launched into a round of balls and teas. A dancing master had been engaged for two afternoons a week to teach her the various dance steps and the hours flew by as she tried to avoid treading on his toes, while Miss May thumped away at the pianoforte.

Marcus Ingram had ordered several gowns from London, finished all but the main seams, and a local dressmaker was brought in to complete them to fit Lucy. These dresses brought home to Lucy the difference between her new life and the old.

She felt exposed in the low-necked evening gowns which showed a great deal of bosom and wondered why such styles should be acceptable when it was considered disgraceful to show an ankle!

'You must never mention the word leg, Lucinda!' Miss May had admonished. 'If you must refer to that part of the body you may say limbs!'

Lucy wondered if this ban applied to the furniture as well, for in many houses the legs of tables and chairs were decently hidden from view. This custom applied in the houses of the well-to-do, of course; the poor had enough trouble keeping themselves clothed, without worrying about the state of their furniture.

'Your papa has accepted an invitation for you to attend a house party at the Appletons' residence,' Miss May announced, all aflutter.

'Who are the Appletons?'

'They live at Hampton House. You must have seen them at church, my dear. Their pew is opposite to ours.'

'A rather plump girl with dark hair, and another one, slightly younger?'

'Those are Miss Appleton and Miss Florence Appleton. There is also a brother, Mr Alfred Appleton, at present home on leave from India. An army officer, of course.'

Seeing that Lucy looked frightened, Miss May hastened to reassure her.

'It will be a small, select party, with dancing. Your papa felt it would make a suitable beginning for you, less of an ordeal than attending a large gathering in the Assembly Rooms in town. That will come later, when you have gained confidence.'

Lucy wasn't so sure about that. In a large ballroom with perhaps a hundred others she could remain anonymous. In a private home she would stand out as the only newcomer, and everyone would know her as the gypsy girl. She was used to being sneered at, of course; she had even had dogs set on her while going from door to door selling clothes pegs and artificial flowers, but this was different. She would be an object of idle curiosity. She said as much to her governess.

Miss May sighed. 'I am well aware that you have had an unfortunate beginning, Lucinda. That cannot now be undone, but my job is to prepare you for the future. You must remember who you are and hold your head high. In any case, your papa and Mr Ivory will accompany us to the party and nobody will dare to treat you rudely while they are present.'

'But you'll be there, won't you?'

'Of course. Strictly speaking, you do not need a chaperone; this is a private party and the men of your family will accompany you, but your papa felt that you might need me there in the background, to advise you if necessary.'

Annie was more excited than Lucy at the thought of the festivities ahead. 'Which gown will you be wearing, Miss? The rose pink moire taffeta, or the green plaid?'

'Make sure that you have them both ready,' Miss May instructed, 'in case Miss Lucinda wants to change her mind at the last minute. Now, Lucinda, you are to go to the study where your papa has taken your mama's jewellery out of the safe. You are to choose what you wish to wear to the Appleton's party. Shall I accompany you, to advise?

★   ★   ★

Jasper had come across the coachman again in the King's Arms. He knew better than to waste money on the man again, but he did sit nearby in case the fellow mentioned anything which might prove useful.

'Got to take the Ingrams over to Appleton's place tomorrow night,' he grumbled, to nobody in particular. 'Hope it's a fine night, that's all I can say. All right for them, inside feasting and dancing, while me and the horses sits outside till lord knows what hour of the morning.'

Jasper's eyes lit up. There would be plenty of comings and goings at this Appleton house, and he might have the chance to get a message to Lucy. Where there was dancing it was quite usual for people to step outside for a breath of fresh air and nobody would think anything of it if she slipped away for a moment or two. That would give him enough time to suggest a meeting in the woods at a later date.

Unfortunately his plans came to nothing. He found the house heavily-guarded with a uniformed footman at every door.

'Nobody in without an invitation,'

one of them informed him haughtily. 'There's been robberies in the district, see, and the Master ain't taking no chances.'

Defeated, Jasper turned away. He was sure he could break in through a window into some darkened room, but he could not afford to take the chance. This was no time to be thrown into gaol while his Lucy needed help.

10

Lucy arrived at Hampton House wearing a new gown and a dark plum coloured cloak, lined with matching satin. In the end she had chosen neither of the evening dresses pressed by Annie, but a white gown daintily embroidered with seed pearls.

Marcus Ingram had decreed that white was the most suitable thing for a young girl at what amounted to her coming-out dance, and Miss May had hastened to do his bidding. Clasped around Lucy's neck was a magnificent blue sapphire pendant which was a family heirloom.

'Good evening, Miss Ingram. So glad you could come.' Lucy's hostess was a plump, middle-aged woman, with what was known as a pouter pigeon bosom. Her gaze raked Lucy from top to toe, but there was obviously nothing she could find fault with so she turned to her son and asked him to introduce Lucy to the other young people.

Captain Appleton was dressed in the red tunic of his regiment, and looked quite handsome, even though his auburn hair clashed with his clothing. 'Charmed,' he said, bending over to kiss Lucy's hand, and she was soon the centre of an admiring throng. That is to say, the gentlemen clustered around her, offering to put their names on her dance card, and the Appleton girls murmured words of welcome, but some of the other young ladies frowned in her direction and whispered things behind their fans.

Lucy's cheeks turned the colour of wild roses that bloomed in the hedge-rows in spring. They surely couldn't be jealous of her, because having dance cards meant that no girl could be a wallflower and no girl could be monopolised by any one man, either. She strongly suspected that her rivals were pointing out the gypsy girl, with varying degrees of scorn.

Miss May took up her position with the chaperones on the chairs against the wall of the ballroom. Perhaps ballroom was a grand name for this chamber of modest size, yet it had clearly been designed as a place for such gatherings, with its crystal chandeliers and the family portraits which graced the walls. Most of the girls wore white and the gentlemen were resplendent in evening dress.

A small orchestra was to provide the music, and its members were already seated on a dais, beginning to tune up their instruments. The candles in the chandeliers and still more which burned in wall sconces lent a soft light which favoured even the plainest of girls.

Miss May was more soberly dressed in dark blue and her only ornament was a gold cross and chain which had belonged to her grandmother. Seated beside a number of sober matrons, who greeted her with pleasant nods, she did not expect to dance but rather to look on. Lucy envied her.

'Is that your cousin, Mr Ivory?' Letitia Appleton whispered. 'He's so handsome, isn't it? You are so lucky to have him for your escort, Miss Ingram.'

'I haven't really thought about it,' Lucy murmured.

'About his looks, or his being your escort?' Letitia giggled.

'I meant his appearance. My Papa came with us, so Ronan is just part of our party. You may have him for yourself if you are so taken with him.'

Letitia slapped Lucy on the arm with her fan. 'Oh, you are naughty, Miss Ingram! How could you say such a thing?' But the considering glance she sent in Ivory's direction made it plain that she was indeed taken with the man.

'And good luck to her,' Lucy thought, holding her head high as she turned to smile at an older man who requested the honour of signing her dance card.

The evening flew by, and to her surprise Lucy found herself enjoying the party. She was a natural dancer and therefore it was easy for her to smile and appear to be responding pleasantly to each of her partners. It was evident to Miss May, looking on, that her charge was the success of the evening.

It was just before the company was to go into supper that things became unpleasant. Lucy had gone to the powder room, which was at some distance from the ballroom, and on the way back she had taken a wrong turning. She could hear music in the distance and on opening a door which she thought might take her in the right direction she found herself in a small balcony, overlooking the billiard room.

Why anyone would want to sit here she had no idea; perhaps it was so that ladies could watch the gentleman playing billiards without actually interrupting them.

She was about to leave when she heard voices below, and she heard her own name. Two men — one of whom was surely Ronan Ivory — were directly beneath the balcony and couldn't see her. She quietly closed the door behind her and sat down to listen.

'Come on, old man,' said the second speaker, whom Lucy didn't know. 'I hate to harry you, but it's about time you paid up. You've kept me waiting for months, and I'm a bit short myself. Can't you at least give me something on account?'

'I'm afraid not at the moment, old boy,' Ivory said airily. 'You know I'll be good for it eventually. Things are just a bit tight at present.'

There was an unpleasant snigger from his friend. 'Better hurry up and marry the heiress, then. Ask Papa for something on account, eh?'

'I have to go carefully,' Ivory admitted. 'Cousin Marcus is all in favour of the marriage, but he says he won't have her forced. She's been through a difficult time, or that's his view of the situation.'

'The girl should be made to toe the line,' the unseen man grunted. 'It was hard luck on you, her turning up like a bad penny when you'd been brought up with expectations. But I can't say I envy you, tied to a gypsy girl like that. How will the county accept her, I wonder?'

'She's not a gypsy!' Ivory snapped. 'You make it sound as if Cousin Marcus had a liaison with a drab and this Lucinda is the result. She was born in holy wedlock, right enough, and stolen by the gypsies. There is a difference.'

'Well, I allow she's pretty enough, Ivory. That should sweeten the blow, I suppose.'

'She's not my type. As soon as I get my hands on her money I'll send her back where she came from. The damn gypsies can keep her, for all I care!'

'I say, old man, that's a bit strong, isn't it?'

Ivory shrugged. 'All my life I've been told that the Briarwood estate was to come to me. Lucinda is the only thing that comes between that and me. She's expendable, Charlie, that's all. There's the gong; we should go to the dining-room, eh?'

Their voices died away, and Lucy leaned back in her chair, stunned. She had been under no illusions that Ronan Ivory loved her, and she had no feelings for him herself. Nevertheless it was horrid to hear him discussing her like this, as if she was an unsatisfactory servant or a pet which had to be put down.

Until now, the choice in her mind lay between returning to her gypsy family, or taking up the life into which she had been born without seeing very far into the future.

She had gathered that she would eventually be expected to take a husband, and that man, whoever he might be, would take up residence with her at Briarwood, whereas most brides were expected to leave home to follow their spouses into whatever world those men chose to lead them.

Lucy had thought of this future husband as some faceless individual, but of course she expected that when he made his appearance he would be kind, and loving and it would all be quite romantic.

Instead, she had encountered one ridiculous proposal from the Reverend Clement Orton, and now this upsetting and rather frightening episode.

She wanted to run away, far from Ronan Ivory and everything he stood for.

The tears rolled down her face as she considered the situation she was in. 'Oh, Jasper,' she whispered, 'where are you? I need you so badly now!'

Lucy crept up to her room, still feeling very upset. There was no doubt in her mind that she would be in trouble when her father came home, not to mention Miss May, so she hoped to be sound asleep before they arrived.

Annie was there, dozing in a chair. She leapt up when the door opened. 'Oh, there you are, Miss. Did you have a lovely time? Have you saved your dance card for your memory box?'

'No, I didn't!' Lucy sniffed. 'Oh, Annie, I was enjoying myself so much, dancing with everyone, and then it all went wrong!'

The practical Annie swept into action at once. 'Let's get them clothes off you, and get you into bed, and then I'll make you some nice hot milk and you can tell me all about it. How will that be?'

Lucy nodded, and by the time she was in her lawn nightgown with all its tucks and lace, she was feeling more relaxed. The promised milk drink arrived soon afterwards and Annie smiled her encouragement as Lucy stammered out her story.

'And of course he doesn't love me at all! He just wants Papa's money!'

Annie shrugged. She had long ago given up trying to fathom the ways of the gentry. 'A lot of folk get married out of convenience,' she said. 'Like my Aunt Patty. She thought she'd never be married, on account of her being so plain, and then a widower chap offered to wed her and she snapped him up at once. Love is for them as can afford it, see? Auntie was getting up in years and didn't want to be an old maid, and her chap was left with three youngsters and a baby when his wife died and he needed another wife, quick sharp.'

'It's not the same thing at all,' Lucy told her, with a catch in her voice. 'I could understand Cousin Ronan wanting to marry for money, but if you could have heard the things he said, Annie! He detests me because I lived with the gypsies, and he means to cast me off as soon as I inherit Briarwood. And you know what the law says; that anything a wife has automatically belongs to her husband. I'd be homeless without a penny to my name!'

'Surely they wouldn't let him do that, Miss?'

'Who are they, Annie? I don't suppose anyone could stop him.'

Annie yawned. 'Well, we can't do

anything about it tonight, Miss, so I suggest you get a good rest. Things will look better in the morning. Should I go along to Miss May and see if she'd like a hot drink? Cook and the others are in bed long since, so she'll get no answer if she rings.'

Lucy's face went red. 'Miss May isn't here, Annie.'

'Not here! Where is she, then?'

'Back at the Appletons' I expect. She'll have to wait until Papa wishes to leave.'

'You mean to tell me you came home all by yourself?'

Lucy nodded. 'I couldn't stay there a moment longer. I ran out to the carriage and got the man to drive me home. He didn't want to leave without Papa's permission, but I made him do it. I know I'll be in trouble in the morning, but I don't care!'

Annie kept her opinions to herself. It was Miss May who would be in trouble, she was sure of that. Mr Ingram would be furious, saying that she was paid to watch over Miss Lucinda and she failed in her duty by letting her run off into the night. The woman might even be dismissed.

Annie climbed into bed, wanting to be well out of the way before the storm broke. As it was she had waited up till all hours for Miss Lucinda to come home, and she was exhausted. For once she looked forward to getting up in the morning. It was to be exciting to see what happened next. A bit of drama was always welcome to break the monotony of everyday life.

As expected, the house was in a turmoil the next morning. As the butler put it, all hell broke loose. He had been jerked out of a sound sleep by the furious jangling of bells and had hastily thrown on some clothes and presented himself to the master. Mr Ingram had been furious, demanding to know why he hadn't been there to greet them, which was totally unfair when he had been told there was no need to stay up, as the gentlemen would see to themselves when they came in.

And of course he hadn't been able to stand up for himself in case he was dismissed for insolence, so he'd had to grovel and say he was very sorry and it wouldn't happen again.

'Well I never!' Cook said. 'Fancy him going on at you like that. It's not like the master to be so cross. Something must have happened.'

'You can say that again! That Miss May was in a right state, wringing her hands and saying she couldn't think how it had happened. She hadn't taken her eyes off Miss Lucinda for a minute but she thought the girl ought to be safe enough going to the powder room without supervision.'

In the midst of all the confusion, nobody noticed when the little maid who had served breakfast to Mrs Ingram and Miss Meech stepped outside to shake the crumbs off their tablecloth. She gave a squeak of alarm when Jasper stepped out of the shadows, putting a finger to his lips as he came.

'Don't run away, Miss, I won't hurt you!' As she hesitated he reached into his pocket and pulled out a note. 'Look, you see that Miss Lucy gets this and I'll buy you a drink in the King's Arms on your next day off.'

'Cook would kill me if I ever went in there,' she muttered, but few girls could resist Jasper's smile and she melted at once.

'All right then, give it here. I'll see what I can do, but no promises, mind! I don't want to lose me job!'

A romantic girl at heart, she assumed that this was Miss Lucinda's lover, forbidden by her father to come to the house. Susie could see why the Miss would be attracted to this man; if she didn't want him, Susie would be the next in line! When she went up to Lucy's room to make the bed she slipped the note under her pillow. It would be a nice surprise at the end of the day.

It was eleven o'clock in the morning before Lucy was summoned to the study to face the music. She found her father pacing up and down in front of the window, Ronan Ivory lounging in a chair with his legs crossed and poor Miss May sitting bolt upright on a hard chair, biting her lip.

'Now then, Miss! What do you have to say for yourself?' Marcus Ingram snapped, without inviting her to sit down. She carefully seated herself on the chair behind her father's desk. It was perhaps inappropriate under the circumstances but she was shaking inwardly and not sure if her legs would hold her up.

'I don't know, Papa,' she faltered.

'You don't know! You're not an idiot, girl! How could you be so careless and rude as to leave the house without thanking your hostess? It created an extremely poor impression, let me tell you! I am sure that over breakfast this morning the Appletons must have been remarking that such behaviour is only to be expected from a young woman who has spent most of her life in gypsy encampments!'

This was a low blow, and Miss May winced. Lucy thought that they were probably saying no such thing. The ladies would still be abed after their late night, and Mr Alfred Appleton had been most kind to her and would be much too polite.

'If you felt unwell, you should have spoken to Miss May and she would have dealt with the situation,' Ingram went on. 'Mrs Appleton would have directed you to a place where you could lie down.'

This gave Lucy a way out, which would have excused her behaviour and, more to the point, relieved poor Miss May of all responsibility. She had only to say that she felt faint and had gone out for a breath of air and then, still feeling ill, had seen the carriage waiting nearby and without thinking had climbed in and directed the coachman to take her home.

Tight lacing often caused ladies to feel faint, so this explanation would defuse the situation. She became aware that Miss May was watching her with hope in her eyes.

Suddenly, anger welled up inside Lucy. It was all Ronan's Ivory's fault, yet there he was, leaning back in that chair, a bored witness to her disgrace. Throwing caution to the winds she burst out with the first words which came to mind.

'I agree I owe you and Miss May an explanation, Papa, but why does he have to be here, taking it all in?'

'Because he is your future husband, Lucinda! That is, if he still wants you after the exhibition you have made of yourself. He intended to speak to you at the ball last night, but your extraordinary behaviour robbed him of the opportunity. Now, what do you have to say about that?'

Did any girl ever have a less romantic proposal of marriage? This would never have happened to one of the heroines in

Miss May's carefully-chosen library books.

Swinging round to face Ivory, Lucy drew herself up to her full height and, looking him right in the eye, gave vent to her feelings. 'I wouldn't marry you if you were the last man on earth, Mr Ivory, so put that in your pipe and smoke it!'

Miss May's mouth opened in a round O of shock but no words came out. Lucy flounced out of the room, ignoring her father's stern demands for her to come back. All Miss May's careful training had fallen by the wayside. She had let poor Miss May down, and she didn't care! She was a strange mixture of gypsy and gentry and there was no help for it. That was all there was to it!

11

Miss May came into the room without bothering to knock, which gave Lucy some indication of how disturbed her governess was.

'Get up at once! No lady sprawls on her bed like an unruly child!'

'I'm not a lady, am I?' Lucy responded, but she got up and sat on the bedside chair, smoothing her skirts as she did so.

'I'm afraid that was painfully obvious this morning, Lucinda. What on earth possessed you to turn on Mr Ivory like that? Have all my lessons meant nothing to you? I can understand that you may not wish to marry him, but a gracious refusal was called for, not that fishwife behaviour. Your papa is most distressed, and rightly so. If only you could have said that you were unwell, you might have been forgiven.'

'Would you have wished me to lie?'

'Of course not, Lucinda, but a little fudging of the facts, perhaps?'

Lucy pointed to the other chair. 'Please sit down, Miss May, I have something to tell you.'

'About the way you spoke to Mr Ivory in such an unfortunate manner?'

'Not exactly, although that was part of it. Please, Miss May.'

The governess sat down and waited. Lucy swallowed hard. 'I went to the powder room, and on the way back I lost my way. I opened the wrong door and found myself on a little balcony, overlooking the billiard room. I heard two men talking, down below. They couldn't see me because I was hidden by the balcony rail.'

'You don't mean to tell me you were eavesdropping, Lucinda?' Miss May was shocked.

'It's a good thing I did. Oh, I didn't mean to at first, but when I heard my name spoken I couldn't resist it. One of the men was Cousin Ronan and the other seemed to be a friend of his, someone who had loaned money to him and wanted it back. To cut a long story short, Ronan Ivory needs money badly and he means to get it by marrying me.'

'Because you are to inherit the Briarwood estates,' Miss May nodded. 'This is not news to me, Lucinda. Your father told me all about it when he first employed me. He knows that you could fall prey to fortune hunters and hopes to see you married as soon as possible to a fine man who will protect you, and manage the estates well when you come into your inheritance.'

'And is he aware that Ronan Ivory has no thought of protecting me, Miss May?' Lucy was unable to keep the bitterness out of her voice. 'He told his friend that he has no love or respect for Papa's gypsy daughter, and will cast me off as soon as he gets his grubby little hands on my money! That is why I spoke as I did.'

'I see.'

Lucy was glad to see that Miss May

believed her, although it would take more than that to make this dilemma go away.

'You must speak to your papa!' Miss May declared. 'He will know what to do next.'

'I'm sure that Cousin Ronan will wriggle out of it somehow. It will be his word against mine. He'll probably suggest that I'm making it all up to get myself out of trouble.'

In her own way, Miss May knew less about the real world than Lucy did. She might have to earn her own living, but she had never run afoul of the peelers or been driven away from farms by people who feared for the safety of their fowls. Outside of the country vicarage in which she had been brought up, most of her knowledge was gleaned from books.

Miss May made up her mind quickly. 'Hurry and put on your bonnet and cloak, my dear, and your outdoor boots. We must leave as soon as possible.'

'Where are we going?'

'To see the vicar. He will know what to do.'

Lucy doubted this, but did as she was told nonetheless. Anything was better than waiting for the blow to fall. The pair hurried off before anyone could see them leaving, and demand to know where they were going. The note from Jasper, which the housemaid had placed under Lucy's pillow, remained there unseen and unread.

'Sorry, Miss, the vicar ain't here. He's gone to see the bishop and isn't expected back until tomorrow morning. If Mr Orton is any use to you, you'll find him in the church.'

Fanny's tone suggested that the curate wasn't likely to be useful to anyone, and as she had a pot on the stove which was likely to boil over at any moment she shut the door and hastened away. At any other time this would have elicited a pithy response from Miss May, who deplored rudeness, but she merely nudged Lucy towards the church, calling out Mr

Orton's name as they approached.

He emerged from the vestry, looking delighted. 'Miss Ingram, Miss May; what a splendid surprise. What brings you here?'

'We need your help, Mr Orton. We are in the most dreadful trouble!'

'You haven't murdered old Mrs Fisher, I trust?' The old lady in question was known as the worst old fusspot in the parish, never grateful for any help she received, and always grumbling about something. Mr Orton raised his eyebrows when his visitors failed to respond to his little joke.

'Lucinda is in danger of being forced into marriage with someone who has evil intentions, and I believe that I am about to be dismissed from my post at the Hall!'

'Dear me, dear me!' Mr Orton was obviously at a loss and no wonder, Lucy thought. Once again she had the feeling that she was an actress playing in a bad farce.

'So are you going to help us, or are

you not?' Miss May demanded.

Her brown eyes were flashing, and Mr Orton gazed at her with interest. How was it that he had never noticed before? He blushed as he remembered Lucy's words to him, when she'd insisted that the governess would make him a better wife than she herself? And now Miss May — Deborah — was in difficulties, and had actually turned to him for help!

'Let us sit down,' he suggested, leading the way to the Lady Chapel. There, while Lucy sat quietly saying nothing, Miss May told the story as she knew it. 'And of course I believe what Lucinda has told me,' she finished, 'but had I heard the tale from anyone else I confess I should not have believed it of Mr Ivory!'

'I fear that gentleman is capable of anything,' Mr Orton replied, 'gentleman being something of a misnomer in his case. Only last week he forced his way into the vicarage and subjected me to a long harangue in front of Mr

Brown! Having learned of my proposal to Miss Ingram he had come to warn me to keep away as he intended to marry her himself. He as good as threatened me with violence should I persist in my suit by speaking to his cousin.'

Kind Mr Orton didn't mention the fact that his vicar, too, had expressed his views on the folly of his aspiring to marry Lucy, and now, seeing Miss May as if for the first time, he understood that it was just as well the proposed engagement had come to nothing. When sufficient time had elapsed he might try to get to know Miss May better, but in the meantime, these ladies needed help, and he must address himself to that.

Darkness had fallen by the time Jasper reached the wood. He hoped that Lucy had received his note and would not have trouble in getting away to meet him. Knowing that it might be difficult, as wealthy people could afford plenty of candles and were therefore likely to sit up late, he was determined to wait all night if need be.

In his mind he had come up with a scenario in which Lucy arrived with a bag containing all her belongings; the pair of them would then mount his horse and ride off into the night, travelling on throughout England and Wales until they found the gypsy band again. Reason told him that this wasn't likely to happen, but it didn't hurt to dream.

Somewhere at the side of the house a door banged, but judging by the snatch of conversation that drifted to him on the breeze it was simply a maid locking up behind a manservant or groom who had gone to the kitchen. Lucy, if she came, would travel quietly, so as to avoid detection.

He stiffened as he saw a light coming from the stable. It appeared to be coming towards the wood. It would of course be sensible for Lucy to have borrowed a lantern; there was no moon and once she crossed the fence the terrain would be rough.

However, as the figure drew closer he realised that the person approaching him was too tall to be Lucy, and furthermore was dressed in an overcoat and narrow trousers. He drew back behind a tree, but the man came straight on without hesitation.

'You may as well come out. I know you're in there somewhere!' the man called, and by the sound of his voice Jasper knew that this was one of the gentry. He stepped forward.

'Mr Ronan Ivory, I believe,' he drawled.

'Yes indeed. And I demand to know who you are, and why you are trespassing here. This is private property.'

'My name is Jem Gates.'

'Ah, yes; the jockey, I believe.'

Jasper bowed an acknowledgement, at the same time feeling in his pocket for a very efficient knuckleduster he kept there. He would only use it in a last resort, but it was as well to be ready to defend himself, as he didn't know what Ivory had in mind.

'I also believe that you are acquainted with the lady I mean to marry, Miss Lucinda Ingram.'

'I've known Lucy all my life,' Jasper told him. 'As for what I'm doing here, I simply want to speak to her.'

'Ah, yes, that much is clear. A note which supposedly came from you was found under her pillow when a maid went to turn down the bed. She was not the person who put it there of course; this one was more loyal and reported her finding to her master at once. Since Miss Ingram is at present away from home in peculiar circumstances, her father took this very seriously and asked me to investigate. I can only say that you are fortunate that he didn't call in the peelers.'

'What circumstances?'

'Not that you have any right to know, but apparently she and her governess are staying at the vicarage, heaven knows why.'

This explained why Lucy hadn't turned up. 'Then I bid you goodnight,' Jasper said, preparing to leave. Much as he would have liked to rearrange Ivory's sneering face he had no wish to get into a fight which would get him into trouble with the law. If he left at once there was every hope that he could speak to Lucy at the vicarage.

'Hold on,' Ivory said. 'I have a suggestion which you might find interesting. Look upon it as a challenge, if you will. Shall we strike a bargain?'

'What sort of challenge?' Jasper felt suspicious of anything this man might have to offer. He didn't trust him in the least.

'I understand you are to ride King's Ransom in the Golden Guineas Stakes next week, and are highly-favoured to win.'

'If your idea is to bribe me to lose the race so you can bet heavily on another horse and win, you can forget about it!' Jasper snapped. 'I mean to back the animal myself.'

'An intriguing notion, but no. I have

167

just purchased a likely runner myself, which goes by the name of Silken Lady. I shall be riding her myself.'

'So?' Jasper had heard via the racing grapevine that Ivory had bought this horse, and as every gentleman was brought up to ride from a very early age, it wasn't unusual for some of them to participate in races as amateurs. Silken Lady was indeed a likely contender and Jasper looked forward to competing against her.

He had no way of knowing that Ivory had not yet paid for the animal but was counting on her to win, at which time he would sell her for more than he had paid. He could then pay his debts with money to spare. However, this was not Ivory's only reason for wanting to win.

'So I suggest we have a little wager, you and I, just to make things interesting. You and I will also be competing against each other, as a race within a race, with the prize being Miss Lucinda Ingram.'

'What!' Jasper couldn't believe his

ears. 'You mean the winner will claim Lucy as his bride? What is in it for you, Ivory? If I beat you, you lose everything.'

'I think not. If I marry her, the Briarwood estate and all her father's wealth will be mine in due course. If you take her away with you, she will lose everything, for her dear papa will hardly wish to endow a lowborn gypsy fellow with the Ingram riches. Cousin Marcus will leave everything to me.'

'You're on!' Jasper said, hesitating not at all. Much as it galled him to do so he thrust out his hand to shake on their pact. The bargain was sealed.

The day of the race dawned fine and clear. The crowd was in good humour, with many people arriving early, to meet their friends and to place their bets.

Stalls had already been set up to sell a variety of goods, and vendors offered food such as baked potatoes, roast chestnuts and sweetmeats.

The racecourse offered no shelter,

apart from a row of open stalls where the horses were tethered, and each trainer had brought a number of grooms to keep an eye on the animals, in case of foul play. Jasper was particularly nervous about King's Ransom. If anything happened to put the horse out of the running, Ivory would win their bet by default.

'You make sure nobody tries to nobble the Ransom,' he ordered, pretending not to notice when the groom thumbed his nose at him as he turned away.

'Don't know who he thinks he is, that ole gyppo,' the groom grumbled, but nobody responded. Both Ned Jarvis and the owner would have their heads if anything happened to the animal, so what Jasper had to say hardly mattered.

The racecourse had been developed for flat racing rather than steeple chasing, but the ground was uneven and the way led across a meadow and through a copse before returning to the starting post, which also served as the finish line. This was a more primitive venue than the well-known racecourses, which had fences to keep back the onlookers, and open stands where they could shelter from the elements.

Jasper was glad of the rough going which he felt gave him an advantage. He had spent his whole life galloping across country and was prepared for anything. Of course, the gentlemen riders were used to hunting, he reflected, so perhaps there was a thin line between them all when it came to experience conditions.

A trumpet call summoned the field to the starting line. Jockeys and horses jostled for position, a pistol cracked, and they were off. Lucy had no idea that her future hung in the balance.

12

The horses thundered around the first bend, with a tall grey in the lead, closely followed by a bay mare ridden by a professional jockey. Jasper and Ivory were riding neck and neck in third place and the rest of the field were strung out behind.

Jasper knew that certain tactics were necessary if he was to win. It was foolish to tire his horse by going to the front of the field too soon in case it flagged within sight of the finish line, but on the other hand he dared not fall behind for fear of being unable to make up the distance at the end. He wished that he had been able to study the form of the participants. He had watched a few of these horses in other races, even ridden against one or two, but there were others which were an unknown quantity.

Then there was Silken Lady. With so much at stake, Ivory wouldn't hesitate to push the poor beast to the limit of her endurance. King's Ransom was fit, and jumping out of his skin with exuberance, but could he match that?

Without warning a dog ran in front of the horses, barking shrilly. The second runner shied and jibbed, lunging into King's Ransom who plunged sideways, almost dislodging Jasper, who managed to hang on. They forged ahead but the small delay had cost them dearly and Silken Lady was now several yards ahead. Ivory looked back, his teeth parted in a triumphant grin. Jasper dug his heels into King's Ransom and managed to lessen the distance between them. Ivory was in second place; Jasper was third.

They were now entering the copse. Ivory and Jasper were riding neck and neck. Then, without warning, Ivory raised his crop and began slashing Jasper over the head and shoulders, opening a thin wound over one eye.

Jasper grimly stayed in place as King's Ransom moved into second place. Ivory now made the mistake of slashing King's Ransom on the flanks, and the animal picked up speed and with no help from Jasper, caught up with the front runner. Any other rider would have fallen off at that point, but Jasper had too much to lose and he clung on grimly. Ivory was left several lengths behind.

A quick glance over his shoulder told Ivory that none of the other riders were in sight, although they would appear at any moment. He made a quick decision. He knew this area well, and if he made a detour he could put himself near the head of the field. All it would take was a dash across a ploughed field, a mighty leap over a stone wall, and he would be back on course again. He pulled the mare's head around and set off.

Ivory was used to hunting and the stone wall presented no challenge to him. Unfortunately the mare had never been hunted, nor was she a steeple-chaser, having been bred solely for racing on the flat. Her owner had planned to race her for a few seasons and then use her for breeding, but financial problems had forced him to sell. When they reached the wall, Silken Lady shuddered to a halt. Ivory was thrown over the obstacle and lay still.

The crowd cheered madly as the horses came into view. There seemed to be little to choose between King's Ransom and the big grey. Within yards of the finish line Jasper and his mount made a superhuman effort and finished first.

When they were led into the roped off area which served as the winner's circle, Jasper slid off the horse and staggered to a stall where he was handed a drink. He felt dazed and his legs seemed to have turned to rubber. He raised a weary hand to brush the blood off his cheek. He seemed to have won, but where was Ivory?

He shook off the congratulations of

Ned Jarvis and the horse's owner. There was only one thing on his mind, and that was to get to Lucy as fast as possible. He wouldn't put it past Ivory, having seen that winning the race was a lost cause, to have reneged on their bargain and gone hotfoot to spirit her away.

Pausing only to ensure that King's Ransom was being properly cared for, he saddled up his own horse and turned his head in the direction of Briarwood Hall. The noise of the crowd faded into the background as she galloped on.

★   ★   ★

'Look after my horse, will you?' Jasper thrust the bridle into the hands of a bewildered groom, who was too taken aback to argue. The butler who answered the front door of Briarwood Hall had his wits about him, but even he was no match for Jasper, who pushed past him, demanding to see Lucy.

It was perhaps fortunate that Marcus Ingram was passing through the entrance hall at that moment, otherwise the butler might have had time to summon help and Jasper would have been ejected.

'You have to listen to me!' Jasper gasped. 'Lucy is in danger!'

'Very well,' Ingram said calmly, ignoring the butler's outraged squawks. 'I'll see you in my study.' Jasper presented a dreadful sight; sweating, mud-spattered, and covered in blood. Yet there was something about him which convinced the magistrate that the fellow had Lucy's best interests at heart. He listened calmly as Jasper gasped out the story of Ivory's scheming.

'I must admit that your story merely confirms what my daughter has already told me,' he said, when Jasper's breath had at last run out. 'She was so distressed that she sought sanctuary at the vicarage, after overhearing a conversation in which my cousin revealed himself to be less than honourable. I have since made inquiries and have been shocked to discover the extent of his debts, not to mention an unfortunate liaison with a village girl which has resulted in the birth of a child. I regret to say that Ronan Ivory is no longer welcome in my house.'

Ingram heaved a sigh as he looked at the drooping figure of his visitor. 'I suppose you'll want to see Lucinda,' he said, after a moment. 'You may wish to er, refresh yourself before I send for her. Someone will take you to a room where you can wash.'

At least he's not sending me out to the yard to put my head under the pump, Jasper thought. That must count for something.

★ ★ ★

Lucy flew into Jasper's arms with a glad cry. 'Oh, Jasper! When Annie came for me I thought it was Cousin Ronan who wanted me. I couldn't bear it, even though Papa told me I didn't have to marry him after all. I hate Ronan Ivory, Jasper, I do really!'

'I don't think he'll trouble you again,' Jasper told her. She listened, open-mouthed, as he told her about the race he had just won.

'Of course, it doesn't mean I have any claim on you, my love,' he said humbly. 'I only agreed to it to save you from Ivory, although I'm not sure he would have abided by our bargain if your father hadn't found him out. All I want is to know that you are safe and happy here. I would never try to take you away from all this.' He waved a hand to encompass the richly-furnished morning room where they were sitting.

Lucy smiled. 'None of this means anything if I can't have you.' She leaned forward and kissed him tenderly, and for a long moment the world seemed to stop turning. How could she ever have contemplated marrying some gentle-man and thereby losing Jasper?

They were interrupted by Miss May, who seemed not to notice that her charge was behaving in a most unlady-like manner, enfolded in the arms of a young man!

'Mr Orton has just arrived with tragic news,' she announced. 'Mr Ivory has been found dead of a broken neck. It appears that he was taking part in a horse race and must have taken a wrong turning, because he was found at some distance from the prescribed course.'

Lucy looked at Jasper in alarm, but he shook his head slightly, to indicate that he was not responsible. At a later date, the coroner would record a verdict of accidental death, saying that horse riding was a dangerous sport and that those who indulged in it knew the risks involved. But on that day Jasper and Lucy had other things to think about, and the most important was to inform her father of her decision to follow her heart.

'I am so very sorry, Papa,' she said, as Miss May looked on, misty-eyed, 'but I've loved Jasper all my life and I know

now that I shall never be contented unless I'm with him. You do understand, don't you?'

Marcus Ingram nodded. 'I cannot pretend to be happy about this, Lucinda, but I will not prevent you from leaving. At least you have been restored to us for a short time, for which I am forever grateful. Never knowing what had become of you would have been agonising. I do insist that you indulge me by marrying in the church here, however. Will you do that?'

So three weeks later Jasper, wearing borrowed finery, met his bride at the altar and they were married. None of their band were present, but as they looked deep into each other's eyes Lucy knew that their friends would be with them when they pledged their love again at the annual gathering of the gypsies.

As they left the church, arm in arm, Lucy tossed her bouquet to Miss May, who managed to catch it. She had lost her job at Briarwood Hall, but was soon to take up another way of life which would suit her much better. She exchanged conspiratorial smiles with the Reverend Clement Orton.

So it was that Jasper rode away from Briarwood Hall with his bride perched behind him. His winnings, combined with money which Lucy's father had pressed upon them, meant that they would not be penniless, but what did they care about that? The love that existed between them was all that they needed, or could ever want.

THE END

We do hope that you have enjoyed reading this large print book.

Did you know that all of our titles are available for purchase?

We publish a wide range of high quality large print books including:
Romances, Mysteries, Classics
General Fiction
Non Fiction and Westerns

Special interest titles available in large print are:
The Little Oxford Dictionary
Music Book, Song Book
Hymn Book, Service Book

Also available from us courtesy of Oxford University Press:
Young Readers' Dictionary
(large print edition)
Young Readers' Thesaurus
(large print edition)

For further information or a free brochure, please contact us at:
Ulverscroft Large Print Books Ltd.,
The Green, Bradgate Road, Anstey,
Leicester, LE7 7FU, England.
Tel: (00 44) **0116 236 4325**
Fax: (00 44) **0116 234 0205**

EACH TIME WE MEET

Marlene E. McFadden

Sarah's new hairdressing salon gives a much-needed boost to her life away from her overbearing ex-boyfriend. Then, she meets Alice, her neighbour — sometimes strange and moody, but also sweet and generous — and is later introduced to her husband, Dr Gareth Bradley. But all is not what it seems, and when Sarah realises she is attracted to Gareth, she discovers how devious Alice can be. Throughout that hot summer of 1955, fear and tension builds within everyone — especially the dedicated, overworked doctor . . .

EDEN IN PARADISE

Joyce Johnson

When Juliette Jordan's parents die at their retirement complex home in Eden Canyon, Arizona, she makes an agonising decision. Knowing their ambitions for her, instead of attending their funeral, she remains in England to attend her interview for a surgical registrar's post. However, calling from Arizona, Josh Svenson criticises her absence and insists that Juliette visit Eden Canyon. She agrees reluctantly, but finds Josh's rudeness unbearable. Then she discovers the shocking truth about her parents . . . but will she also find love?